*For the other Tucker*

Behold, I was shapen in iniquity; and in sin did my mother conceive me.

—PSALM 51

# PART ONE
# THE SWING

During the latter years of the Postdigital Age, discorporeal Klaatu artist Iyl Rayn attempted to enhance her status within the Cluster by conceiving an unconventional entertainment. She contracted the services of certain Boggsian corporeals to construct a network of portals, or as she called them, diskos.

The diskos were designed to transport small quantities of coherent information from one geotemporal location to another. In short, they allowed any discorporeal being to displace itself in time and space.

The inspiration for Iyl Rayn's effort was an ancient and largely discredited discipline once known as History. Each of her diskos led to one or more specific events that she deemed relevant. Iyl Rayn hoped that her portals would convince other Klaatu to share her fascination with corporeal human accomplishments such as the ascent of Mount Everest, the invention of movable type, and the construction of the Lah Sept pyramid at Romelas. She also found cause for fascination in disasters such as the bombing of Hiroshima, the onset of the Digital Plague, and the Martian Biocide.

Most Klaatu considered themselves to be above showing interest in such trivialities. However, they were not immune to novelty's lure, and Iyl Rayn's efforts enjoyed an intense, though brief, period of popularity.

It was soon discovered that a design flaw in the Boggsian-built diskos permitted their use by corporeal entities, thus introducing physical anachronisms into the time streams. The majority of Klaatu, who regarded corporeals as lesser creatures, abandoned the diskos and turned to more refined perceptual manipulations, leaving Iyl Rayn to contemplate the consequences of her creation.

The diskos themselves remained in place, unused except by those hapless creatures who stumbled into them by chance and so found themselves transported.

— **E**[3]

# 1  THE WOODEN TROLL

THE FIRST TIME HIS FATHER DISAPPEARED, TUCKER FEYE had only just turned thirteen.

That morning, he had been amusing himself by building a simple catapult—a wooden plank balanced across an old cinder block—in the backyard. He placed a stone at one end of the plank, climbed onto the seat of his dad's lawn tractor, and jumped down onto the other end of the plank. The stone hopped vigorously from the far end, but not very high. Thinking maybe he wasn't jumping hard enough, Tucker moved the catapult over by the garden shed. He found an old toy metal fire truck he would never play with again and set it on the end of the plank.

A fire truck needed a fireman. Tucker went into the house to find one of his old toy soldiers, but then he remembered he'd given them away for the spring rummage sale at his dad's church. All he could find was a six-inch-tall wooden troll that his dad had carved as a boy. The troll had been standing guard over the bookcase in the living room ever since Tucker could remember. He took the figurine outside and wedged it into the fire truck. He then climbed onto the roof of the shed.

It took him a few moments to gather his courage. Finally, after a few false starts, he jumped. His feet struck the end of the plank perfectly. The fire truck leaped from the end of the plank, flew through the air, and landed on the house, tearing loose a shingle as it tumbled down the steep roof.

Tucker quickly retrieved the truck from his mother's herb garden and disassembled the catapult. The wooden troll was nowhere to be found. When his mom came out and asked him about the noise, he told her a blue jay had hit the window and flown away.

She crossed her arms and gave him a skeptical look.

"Must have been a big jay," she said.

Tucker grinned and shrugged. His mom managed to hang on to her stern expression for a few seconds, then grinned back at her son, shook her head in mock frustration, and went back inside.

The Reverend Adrian Feye had performed a baptism that morning at the Holy Word, his small ministry in downtown Hopewell, Minnesota. The boy child was christened Matthew, a good biblical name of which the Reverend approved. After the baptism he walked home alone, a twenty-minute journey. As he came up the long driveway, he noticed the loose shingle on the roof.

The Reverend stood frowning for a few seconds, wondering how the shingle had become damaged, and why he had not noticed it before. When the answer did not come to him, he sought out his son, Tucker, whose name was nowhere mentioned in the Bible. He found him in the garage fixing a flat tire on his bicycle.

"Tuck?"

Tucker looked up. He could see in his father's features the man he would someday become—the long jaw; the small, bright blue eyes; the wide mouth—but their differences were equally striking: the Reverend's creased face and graying hair made him look older than his forty-two years, and the set of his mouth gave him a perpetually disapproving air, whereas Tucker seemed always to be on the verge of an impish grin.

"Something tore a shingle off the roof," said the Reverend. He waited for Tucker to incriminate himself.

In that moment, Tucker almost confessed, but something about the way his father crossed his arms—the way he seemed to already have found him guilty—caused Tucker to deny all knowledge of the damaged roof.

"Maybe it came off in that storm last week," Tucker suggested.

His father gave him a piercing look.

Tucker put on his innocent face, committed to his lie.

After several seconds that seemed to last for minutes, the Reverend shook his head and muttered, "As thy children are conceived in sin, so shall sin conceiveth in their hearts."

Tucker had heard him say such things before. He had stopped taking it personally. His father quoted scripture the way other people breathed the air. Tucker watched him go into the house. A few minutes later, his father reappeared in jeans and a blue flannel shirt. He fetched the extension ladder from the shed and leaned it against the eave. Tucker offered to help, but his father refused.

"It's too steep, Tuck. Where there is one loose shingle, there may be others. I don't want you falling off the roof."

Tucker felt bad that his dad had to climb up on the roof. He promised himself that he wouldn't tell any more lies for the rest of the week, then went out back to dig some bait from the compost pile. The pond behind the house was good for catching bullheads and perch. Tucker had just found his first angleworm when he heard a startled exclamation. He looked up to see his father standing at the peak, holding a small object in his hand.

The wooden troll.

Tucker ducked behind the shed. How could he explain how the troll had gotten on the roof? He would have to confess. He was not afraid of physical punishment—the Reverend was severe, but he would never lay a hand on anyone. What Tucker feared was the look of weary and profound disappointment his father would lay upon him, more painful than any beating.

He was trying to think how to phrase his confession when his thoughts were shattered by his father's scream—more of a hoarse shout—cut off just as it reached the high point. Tucker ran back around the shed and looked up.

The roof was empty, except for something hovering just off the edge. It looked like a thin, perfectly round disk of wavery glass, about four feet in diameter, hanging in midair. As he watched, the disk faded, then vanished completely.

Tucker ran toward the house, his eyes raking the ground, expecting to find his father, but he was nowhere in sight. He circled the house, looking up, looking down, calling out for his father. He ran to the back door and shouted through the screen, "Mom! Come quick!"

His mom came running up from the basement, a full laundry basket in her arms. "What? Are you all right?"

"Dad fell off the roof!" Tucker pointed up.

The laundry basket dropped from her hands and rolled, spilling a ragged line of wet undergarments across the kitchen floor. She ran out the door, looking left and right, her long, reddish-orange hair whipping back and forth. "Where? Where is he?" She ran around the house with Tucker following closely.

"He was fixing a shingle, then he yelled and he was gone," Tucker said.

His mother stopped running and looked at the ladder leaning against the eaves. She took a shaky, calming breath. "Honey, maybe he walked into town for some supplies."

"No! I'm telling you! He was up there, and he yelled, and he was gone. And I saw something up there."

"Saw what?"

"I don't know. It was round." He pointed up at the roof. There was nothing there.

His mother put her hands on his shoulders. Her eyes, sometimes blue and at other times green, searched his face. "Maybe he went over to the Reillys' to borrow a tool. People do not just disappear, Tucker."

"Yeah, well, he *did* disappear."

"I'm sure he'll be home soon." She went back into the kitchen and began picking up the spilled laundry. Tucker stood outside, watching her through the screen door. Had he imagined it? He didn't think so. Maybe his dad had fallen off the roof, banged his head, and run off into the woods . . . but that didn't explain the disk he had seen. He walked around the house again and again, looking for any sign of his father hitting the ground, but found no trace of him.

# 2  LAHLIA

Tucker's mother was proven correct. An hour later, the Reverend came walking up the long driveway. He was not alone. Beside him was a slim, pale girl with hair the yellow-white of corn silk.

Tucker ran to him.

"Dad! Where'd you go? Are you okay?"

"I'm fine, Tuck." The Reverend Feye clasped the boy to his hip with one arm, then released him. Tucker looked from his father to the girl, then back to his father.

"Tucker, this is Lahlia," said the Reverend.

The girl might have been anywhere between ten and fourteen years old. She wore a slightly torn and smudged shift made of material that shone like silver foil but draped like fine fabric. Her feet were covered with what looked like bright blue painted-on stockings. In her arms she held a small gray cat.

"Hi," said Tucker.

Lahlia stared at him with the biggest, blackest eyes Tucker had ever seen. She looked frightened. Tucker looked to his father for an explanation, but the Reverend stood gazing at the house, lips parted, eyes moist. The clean jeans and blue flannel shirt he had been wearing an hour earlier were dirty. One knee was torn open. His skin was a shade darker, and the lines radiating from the corners of his eyes appeared deeper, as if he had spent hours squinting under a hot sun. His feet were covered by skintight blue sheaths identical to those worn by the girl.

"What's on your feet?" Tucker asked.

His father looked down. "I lost my shoes."

"What happened to you? You look different."

"We'll talk about it later," he said. "Let's go see your mother."

Tucker followed Lahlia and his dad into the house, where his mom was sitting on the sofa, reading a book. She looked up, set the book down, and smiled.

Unlike the Reverend's grim, flat smile, Emily Feye's smile transformed her face and brought light into the room. She stood up and kissed her husband on the cheek. He put his arms around her and hugged her, burying his face in her hair.

"Emily," he said. He held her as both Tucker and Lahlia stared at them. Tucker was surprised—his dad was not usually so demonstrative. After a few seconds, his mother gently broke the embrace and gave her husband a searching look.

"Where have you been?" she asked.

"I had to . . . I had to run into town."

Emily Feye frowned, waiting for more, her eyes moving from his face to his tattered clothing and back again.

The Reverend put a hand on the girl's shoulder. "This is Lahlia. She'll be staying with us for a while."

"My goodness," Tucker's mother said, her puzzled frown becoming a puzzled smile. She knelt down to face the girl. "Where ever did you come from?"

Clutching the kitten to her chest, Lahlia stepped back, bumping against the Reverend's leg.

"There's nothing to be afraid of," Emily Feye said.

Lahlia stared back at her and swallowed. The kitten yawned.

"Such a cute kitty. Look at those big yellow eyes."

The Reverend said, "Lahlia is an orphan. She is from . . . Bulgaria. I don't think she speaks much English."

"An orphan! Oh, dear!" Emily Feye looked at Lahlia, then back at her husband with a slight frown. "From *Bulgaria*?"

"We can talk about it later," the Reverend said. It was the same thing he had said to Tucker—his way of saying, *I don't want to talk about it at all.* Or maybe this time he was saying, *Not in front of Tucker and the girl.*

Tucker's mother put on a bright smile for the girl's benefit. "What *interesting* clothing," she said, fingering the edge of Lahlia's tattered shift. "I had a silver-colored dress when I was a little girl. What is your kitten's name, sweetie?"

"Lahlia," the girl said, pronouncing it *lah-LEE-uh.*

Tucker's mother smiled. "So you can speak! Your kitten's name is the same as your name?"

11

Lahlia shook her head and pointed at herself. "Lahlia."

"I don't think she likes being called *sweetie*," Tucker said.

"Oh! I'm sorry. *Lahlia.* That's a nice name."

Tucker's father cleared his throat. "I'm going to change clothes. Perhaps you could find something more appropriate for her to wear?" Without waiting for an answer, he left them and went upstairs.

"I think some of Tucker's old things will fit you," Emily Feye said. "I'll see what I can find. Then we'll have some cookies. Do you like cookies?"

Lahlia nodded. It was not clear whether she understood the question or was simply trying to be agreeable.

"Back in a jiffy." Emily Feye opened the basement door and trotted downstairs, where she kept boxes of clothes Tucker had grown out of. Tucker, not sure what to do, stood looking at Lahlia.

The girl's dark eyes flickered across the sofa, the easy chair in the corner, the coffee table, the pictures on the walls. *She* is *very odd looking,* Tucker decided. *Not exactly pretty, but interesting.*

He said, "So how'd you . . . uh . . . What are . . . What are you doing here?"

Lahlia stared back at him with an intensity that made his skin prickle.

"Can you speak English?" Tucker asked.

Lahlia did not say anything.

Uncomfortable with her staring silence, Tucker took a step back. Lahlia followed him with her eyes.

*"Tuckerfeye,"* the girl said.

Tucker wasn't sure he'd heard her right.

"Just Tucker," he said.

Lahlia nodded. *"Tuckerfeye,"* she said again, then walked over to the easy chair and sat down with the cat on her lap. Both Lahlia and the cat kept their eyes locked on Tucker. He stood there feeling stupid for as long as he could stand it, then said, "Excuse me," and ran up the stairs to his parents' bedroom.

His father was sitting on the edge of the bed, peeling off the blue foot coverings. His feet were as white as a bullhead's belly.

"Dad?"

"What is it, Tuck?"

"Where did you go? I mean, really."

The Reverend looked at Tucker. He seemed about to say one thing, hesitated, then said, "I just came up here to change."

"I mean *before*. You were on the roof, and you yelled, and all of a sudden you were gone."

"I went downtown." He squeezed the blue foot coverings into a surprisingly small ball and dropped them into the wastebasket.

"You disappeared!"

"Maybe it seemed that way, Tuck. I—ah—I remembered suddenly that I had to run into town. That's where I picked up Lahlia."

"After you disappeared, I saw something on the roof. Like a disk."

The Reverend took a moment to reply. "Probably just heat distortion from the hot sun."

Tucker sensed he was being lied to, and it frightened him. He watched as his dad put on a clean pair of jeans and a flannel work shirt.

"You look different," Tucker said.

"People change, Tuck."

"Yeah, but not like *that*. Not that fast."

His father regarded him for several silent seconds, his face growing hard. "Why don't you go see what the girl and your mother are up to, Tuck," he said at last, making it clear from his tone that the subject was closed.

Minutes later, the Reverend was back on the roof pounding nails, finishing the job he had started that morning. Lahlia and Tucker's mom were in the kitchen eating cookies. Tucker went outside to finish fixing his bike tire and contemplate his father's odd behavior.

The strangest part of it all—his dad never said a word about the wooden troll.

That evening, they sat down to a meal of roast pork, boiled new potatoes, and fresh peas from the garden. Tucker's mom opened a can of tuna for the kitten. They sat at the kitchen table, hands folded, waiting for the Reverend to say grace. The Reverend picked up his knife and fork and looked at each of them in turn.

"There will be no more praying in this house." He gave them a few seconds to absorb that, then said, "It's all lies."

It felt to Tucker as if a smothering mist had descended upon them. The act of breathing became a conscious effort.

Tucker's mother put her hand to her heart. "Adrian . . ."

"There is no God," said the Reverend Feye, serving himself a slice of pork. "And that is all I have to say on the matter."

Lahlia, wearing Tucker's old Mickey Mouse T-shirt, smiled uneasily. Tucker stared at his father, waiting for him to make it into a joke—except his father rarely joked, and never about God.

The Reverend began eating. Tucker looked to his mother, who, with a grim set to her mouth, began to serve herself and Lahlia.

They ate their meal in silence. Only Lahlia, who refused the pork but fell eagerly upon the fresh peas and new potatoes, seemed to enjoy the unblessed food.

**3 FAITHLESS**

AFTER SUPPER, AS HIS MOM MADE UP THE GUEST BED FOR Lahlia, Tucker retired to his own room. He tried to read a book about submarines, but couldn't focus. There was too much strangeness in the house. He lay in bed, staring up at the cracks on his ceiling, trying in vain to understand what had happened that day.

Eventually, he fell into a troubled sleep and dreamed of a strange silent girl with eyes as black as charcoal. He was awakened around midnight by the muffled sound of his parents' voices coming from their bedroom. He couldn't understand what they were saying, but his mom's voice had a strident tone, while his father's preacherly drone came through like white noise. He pressed his ear to the wall.

". . . then Tucker said you fell off the roof, and the next thing I know, you've brought that little girl home. What am I supposed to think?"

"I'm sorry, Em. I can't explain it. Maybe I did fall off the roof. Maybe I was confused and walked in to town. It's not important."

"Not important? You bring a strange girl into our home and it's not *important*?"

"I don't mean it like that. Of course it's important. We'll find a home for her soon."

"Yes, but who is she? Where did she come from?"

There was a long silence, then his father spoke.

"I don't know. I found her wandering around downtown. She wouldn't speak except to tell me her name."

"You should have called the sheriff."

"I notified them, but they won't find her parents."

"How can you know that?"

"Trust me. She is an orphan, abandoned by her parents. Like you," his father said in a softer voice.

Again, a long silence.

"Do you remember anything about that, Em? About before you were adopted?"

"Nothing real," said Emily Feye.

Tucker knew that his mom was adopted, and that she had never found out who her birth parents were. He had never thought about it much — it was a fact of life. His mom had told him that Hamm and Greta Ryan, an older, childless couple, had found her crying outside the boarded-up Hopewell House hotel when she was no more than four years old. Unable to find out where she had come from or who her parents were, they had adopted her. Both Hamm and Greta had died of natural causes shortly after Tucker was born — he didn't remember them at all, but his mother spoke of them fondly and often.

Tucker sat with his ear to the wall for several more minutes. Except for a few soft murmurs, he heard nothing more.

The Reverend Feye delivered his usual Sunday service the next morning, saying nothing of his loss of faith. In his sermon, he railed against avarice and fornication, somehow connecting the two. He related the Parable of the Sower, and he urged his parishioners to find a good home for the orphan Lahlia, who was sitting in the front pew next to Tucker.

Emily Feye played the enormous pipe organ, as always, her feet working the pedals, hair bouncing as she leaned this way and that, reaching across the wide console to finger the ivory and teak keys. Her prowess on the organ was local legend, and many came just to watch her perform.

Shortly after Tucker's parents had married, his father had found the pipe organ stored in an abandoned church near Decorah, Iowa. The two hundred twelve pipes, some as tall as sixteen feet, had been tarnished and clogged with rodent nests, many of the pedals and keys were missing or broken, the wind chests were badly cracked, and the electric bellows did not work at all.

Certain he could repair the organ, he purchased it for six hundred dollars, hauled it back to Hopewell, rented a vacant building downtown, and set about restoring the neglected instrument.

Because the Reverend had no training as a musician or as an organ restorer, he accidentally reversed the order of the foot pedals and transposed several of the pipes. Most of the original ivory keys were damaged; these he replaced with dark, polished teak. The final result, while magnificent in appearance, was unsettling to Alvina Johanson, who had played a smaller organ for a church in Lanesboro. When Alvina sat at the console and attempted a rendition of "Holy, Holy, Holy," what she got instead was a herd of trumpeting elephants and howling tom-cats. She snatched her fingers from the keyboard and pushed herself back with a look of horror. "This is not an organ," she declared. "It is an instrument of audial torture!"

"Perhaps you are not playing it correctly," suggested Emily Feye, leaping to her new husband's defense.

"Fiddlesticks!" Alvina declared. "No sane person could play this cursed device!"

Emily Feye, who was by then pregnant with Tucker, stub-bornly set about mastering the instrument. As she slowly learned her way around the misplaced keys and pedals, sounds mournful and joyous, strident and passionate, shivered the thin walls of the fledgling church. Meanwhile, Adrian set to work installing several rows of pews, a small altar of limestone and oak, and a set of stained-glass windows he had scavenged from an abandoned Catholic church in Zumbrota. Shortly thereafter, he announced the opening of the Church of the Holy Word.

The young Reverend's passion, the impressive pipe organ, and the lack of alternative entertainment drew people from all over Hopewell County and beyond. Worshippers traveled from as far away as Austin to hear Adrian Feye speak the Word of God, and to watch the preacher's pregnant wife operate the largest pipe organ in seven counties.

Several times during the service, Tucker felt Lahlia looking at him. He liked that she found him so interesting, but at the same time, it made him uncomfortably self-conscious. He kept his eyes on the front of the church and refused to look back at her.

After the service, the Reverend performed another baptism, then counseled a young couple on their plans for marriage, prescribing fidelity, commitment, and haste — this last because the bride-to-be was looking suspiciously plump around the middle. He acted in every way like the same devout country preacher the people of Hopewell expected: spiritually fundamentalist, but practical in matters of the flesh.

If any of the parishioners noticed anything different about the Reverend Feye, they said nothing. Where preachers were concerned, few of the faithful saw beyond the collar.

For several more days, Lahlia remained a mute, wide-eyed presence in the Feye household. Tucker found the girl fascinating to look at, but intolerable to be looked at *by.* Her eyes were rapacious, devouring whatever they fell upon. Every time he caught her staring at him, he felt as if she were sucking the color right out of his skin.

The gray kitten was with her always, either in her arms or following at her heels. One afternoon, while lying on his belly at the end of the dock trying to catch minnows with one of his mother's kitchen strainers, Tucker felt a cool shadow cross his back. He rolled onto his side and looked up to find Lahlia's eyes fixed upon him.

"Hi," he said.

Lahlia stared.

"I'm catching minnows," Tucker said.

Lahlia blinked and stared.

Tucker had tried staring her down once. It was not an experience he cared to repeat. He returned to his work, holding the strainer in the water and waiting for an unwary minnow to swim into it. The back of his neck prickled with the girl's presence. He stood it for about half a minute, then whirled on her and shouted, "What?"

Startled, Lahlia stepped back and lifted her hands as if to fend off an attack. When Tucker didn't move, she blinked, flooding both cheeks with tears.

Tucker, feeling bad about scaring her, said, "Are you okay?"

Lahlia turned and walked slowly back through the trees toward the house, followed closely by her cat.

\*　\*　\*

Arnold and Maria Becker, an older couple who ran a small dairy farm two miles outside of Hopewell, agreed to adopt Lahlia. The Beckers were among the most devout and rigid of Tucker's father's parishioners; they possessed both a strong sense of duty and a surplus of household tasks. Tucker watched from his bedroom window as his father led Lahlia out of the house to Arnold Becker's aging pickup truck. She was wearing a pair of Tucker's old jeans, a bright red T-shirt, and flip-flops from the Economart. She had no bag; she owned nothing other than the little cat in her arms. As they drove off, Tucker allowed himself to imagine that everything would go back to normal. Maybe Lahlia had been responsible for his father's peculiar behavior and loss of faith. Maybe, now that she was gone, he would start acting like himself again.

Over the following days and weeks, Tucker watched his father for signs of change, but the Reverend stayed the course. He did not say grace that night, nor on any subsequent night. He preached every Sunday. He officiated at baptisms and weddings, visited parishioners who were ill or injured, and continued to wear his collar.

In this way, the summer passed quickly. Tucker occupied himself by fishing and exploring the countryside with Will and Tom Krause, who lived a mile up the road. As long as he stayed busy he didn't have to think too much about his father's peculiar transformation.

He did often find himself thinking about Lahlia, though. He wondered what her life was like now. Had she learned to talk? Did she still have that little gray cat? He saw her at church on Sundays, sitting in the back pew squeezed between Arnold and Maria, but he had not tried to speak with her. He still associated Lahlia with his father's loss of faith, even though he knew that wasn't fair. How could a young girl make a preacher give up on God? It made no sense. But he thought about her—a lot. Those few days when she had stayed with them had been uncomfortable and strange, but he missed having her around. Sometimes he felt as if she was watching him. He would turn around, but there would be no one there.

Neither of his parents seemed happier without God in the house. His dad became moody and withdrawn. The Reverend Feye was not a naturally affectionate person, but he had always made an effort—a pat on the head or shoulder, and, once in a while, an awkward, bony hug. Tucker always felt that the gestures were not quite real, as if something had clicked in his father's mind saying, "Give boy affection." Still, Tucker craved those touches, which the new, godless version of Reverend Feye dispensed with ever increasing frugality.

The long hours the Reverend had once spent reading the Bible and other religious texts became devoted to his childhood pastime of carving wooden figurines, a hobby he now resumed with grim intensity. Before long, the house teemed with gnomes, dwarves, and trolls carved from the roots of a cottonwood that had fallen in a windstorm. Every table, shelf, nook, and cranny soon hosted one or more of the Reverend's timber creations, all of which were possessed of a scowling, joyless demeanor.

But the change was hardest on Tucker's mother. While she still prayed and read her Bible every night, she did so alone and cheerlessly. She attended Sunday services and played the organ, but something had gone out of her performance—hymns that had once felt jubilant and lively took on a desolate, melancholy air.

At home she read for hours, mostly novels about faraway times and places. "One day," she told Tucker, "I'm going to return to school and study the history of all the world." She became addicted to sudoku puzzles. She bought books filled with the vexing number grids and worked one puzzle after another. Tucker tried one of the simpler ones. It was worse than doing math homework. He took the unfinished grid to his mother, who was sitting on the porch working her own puzzle.

"Think of the numbers as people," she said. "Five is a boy like you, made up of two and three. Nine is your father, five plus four, or two plus seven. Seven is a happy girl—you can see her smile. And when all the numbers come together, it is a prayer I send to God."

Tucker laughed because he did not know how else to respond. His mother returned to her puzzle, and Tucker went to sit on the porch and think. *Numbers were people? Prayers were numbers?* It made no sense at all.

But then nothing made sense. Could both of his parents be right about God? Since God was omnipotent, could he make himself nonexistent for some people while remaining real for others? The thought was simultaneously disturbing and reassuring; Tucker did not dwell upon it for long.

Toward the end of summer, the Beckers stopped attending the Holy Word and began attending a more rigorously religious Baptist church in a nearby town. Tucker missed seeing Lahlia at Sunday worship. He missed her eyes on him. He hoped to see her again when school started in September. In the meantime, he spent as much time as he could outside, away from the doleful cloud that hovered over his home.

It was several months before he realized that his mother was losing her mind.

# 4 EXTINCTIONS

In September, Tucker entered the eighth grade at Hopewell Public. He looked for Lahlia every day, but she never appeared at school. Tucker asked Tom Krause, who lived near the Becker place, if he had heard anything about her.

"That yellow-haired girl?" Tom said. "I think they're home-schooling her because of what happened with Ronnie."

"Who's Ronnie?"

"Ronnie Becker. The Beckers' son. He was growing marijuana behind their barn and getting in all kinds of trouble. He ran off about fifteen years ago and never came back. That's how come they're homeschooling the new girl—to keep her away from bad influences."

"Bad influences like you?"

Tom laughed and faked a punch at Tucker. "Bad influences like your uncle. That's who Ronnie Becker ran off with."

Tucker was so surprised he didn't know what to say. He knew that he had an uncle Curtis who lived someplace in Wisconsin, but he had never met him. His dad never talked about him.

"Who told you that?"

"My dad remembers when it happened. Ronnie and your uncle quit high school and took off."

Tucker absorbed this new information about his family.

Tom said, "Anyway, I guess the Beckers aren't taking any chances with the girl."

Tucker said, "You think she's pretty?"

"Pretty *funny* looking!" Tom laughed.

"Do you ever see her?"

"I went over there once, to return some tools my dad borrowed. She was playing with a kitten."

"She say anything?"

"I think she said hi or something. She talks kind of strange." Tom gave Tucker a sideways look. "Why? You got a thing for her?"

"No!"

"I bet you do," said Tom.

Tucker shook his head. "She's from Bulgaria," he said. "I just wanted to ask her what it was like."

That night, Tucker decided to ask his dad about the uncle he had never met.

"Is it true Uncle Curtis dropped out of school and ran off with Ronnie Becker?"

His father set down the troll he had been carving. "Who have you been talking to?"

"Tom Krause. He says his dad told him."

The Reverend nodded slowly. "It is true. Curtis was a hellion. It was my fault, I suppose."

"Why?"

The Reverend's mouth tightened, then relaxed. "You know my parents died young, Tuck. Your grandmother died giving birth to Curtis. He never knew her. Our father died when Curtis was ten. I was nineteen. Those were hard times. I was not equipped to raise a boy, especially not a boy as wild and rebellious as Curtis. I spent all my time studying the Bible and learning ancient languages, while he practically lived in the garage, working on his motorbike. I was so obsessed with my work that I had no time for him. When he was seventeen, I made my pilgrimage to the Holy Land and left him on his own for a few months. That was a mistake. When I returned home, my brother was a changed person. We fought, and he left. He hasn't been back since."

"When was that?"

"A few weeks before your mother and I married." His eyes softened. "That was a remarkable year. It was the same year I founded my church, the year you were born. . . ." A wry smile creased his face. "On the day you were born—that was the day Lorna Gingrass ran into those pigeons." He shook his head slowly. "I was so young and foolish, I thought it was a sign from God."

Tucker had heard the pigeon story many times before. It was the most famous event in Hopewell history. Lorna Gingrass, Hopewell's only hairdresser, had been driving to work when two large birds struck her windshield. Lorna pulled over and ran back to the grassy ditch where they had landed. One bird was clearly dead. The second bird was stunned but alive, its red eyes blinking. She decided to leave it, hoping it would recover on its own.

Later, at the beauty shop, Lorna happened to mention the sad event while cutting Minna Jensen's hair.

"What kind of birds were they?" Minna asked. She was an avid bird-watcher.

"Sort of gray, with a reddish breast," said Lorna.

"Like a hawk?" Minna asked, thinking they might be kestrels.

"More like big pigeons," said Lorna.

Minna could not imagine what sort of birds they could be. Perhaps some unfamiliar breed of domestic pigeon? She asked Lorna to drive her out to look at the mystery birds.

It took some time—one spot on the highway looked much the same as another—but eventually Lorna located the dead bird. Minna carefully lifted it from its resting place. Her heart began to pound.

"I must be dreaming," she said.

"What is it?" Lorna asked.

"It looks," Minna said slowly, "like a passenger pigeon."

Lorna said, "Didn't they all die out a hundred years ago?"

Minna nodded, then shook her head in disbelief. "You said one of them was still alive?"

They found the second bird a few yards away, its red eyes dull, dry, and unblinking. It had not survived.

Minna's field identification of the birds was quickly confirmed by an ornithologist: they were passenger pigeons, a male and a female. Once the most numerous bird in North America, passenger pigeons had been thought extinct since 1914. The story was picked up by CNN, and the area around Hopewell was suddenly teeming with camera crews, news vans, and bird-watchers.

Hopewell House, the four-story hotel in downtown Hopewell that had been vacant for several years, was hastily refurbished and reopened. For several months, it remained at full capacity, filled with birders and ornithologists. Red's Roost, the only bar in town, did a banner business, especially after Red Grauber renamed it the Pigeon Drop Inn and added a specialty martini called the Drunken Pigeon to the menu.

But the excitement faded over the next months when no other passenger pigeons were seen. Lorna Gingrass had apparently killed the last—and only—pair. Hopewell House once again closed its doors, and the passenger pigeon story faded from the national memory.

*   *   *

The Reverend chuckled, a sound Tucker hadn't heard in weeks.

"I sometimes think those two birds were Hopewell's last gasp," he said. "It's been downhill for this community ever since."

Tucker didn't want to talk about pigeons. He wanted to talk about his uncle.

"Do you ever talk to him?" he asked. "Uncle Curtis?"

His father's smile flattened. "I failed Curtis, son. But some things, like the passenger pigeons, are best left buried in the past." He picked up the troll and went to work on its eyes.

# 5 GHOSTS

As the weather turned cold and Tucker spent more time at home, he began noticing a number of disturbing changes in his mother—little things at first, such as turning light switches on and off several times, and washing clean clothes over and over again, and making strange, repetitive movements—she would sit in her favorite chair and flop her head back and forth, or flap her hands as if she was trying to air-dry them. She carried a book of sudoku puzzles with her everywhere, and seemed content only when filling in grids.

Anything new or unexpected would upset her—loud noises, a surprise visitor, or even a rearrangement of furniture. One day, Tucker pulled the sofa out from the wall to get a book that had fallen behind it and neglected to push the sofa back in place. When his mom came into the room and noticed the sofa out of place, she started flapping her hands, then ran upstairs to her room and rolled herself up in her comforter. She stayed like that until Tucker's dad got home and coaxed her out of her improvised cocoon.

Such episodes came more and more frequently. She kept the window shades pulled down, claiming that she did not care to be "watched like some bug in a bottle." She lost weight, and her already light skin grew paler from lack of sunlight. Her once warm and strong voice became hesitant and quavery. Her hair began to change color, emerging brittle and white without bothering to pause at gray. Some days she would sit brushing it, counting the strokes, until it crackled with static electricity and stood out from her head in a pale, orange-tipped nimbus.

Her organ playing deteriorated as well. Her hands would jitter across the keys, producing a cacophony of raucous bleats and howls that caused Mrs. Iverson's one-year-old to cry. One day she refused to play the instrument at all, claiming that the pipes were sucking her soul out through her fingertips.

The Reverend persuaded Alvina Johanson to make another effort to learn the eccentric ways of the instrument. Soon, Alvina's approximations of "Abide with Me" and "Amazing Grace" filled the church as Emily Feye sat with Tucker in the front pew with her crackling hair and distant smile, working a sudoku puzzle.

Tucker's father took her to several doctors. Harmon Anderson, their family doctor in nearby Chalmers, referred her to a neurologist in Minneapolis. The neurologist referred her to a psychiatrist. Their diagnoses ranged from depression to schizophrenia to chronic fatigue syndrome. They prescribed a panoply of drugs, but nothing helped. Finally, in November, Tucker and his father took her to the Mayo Clinic in Rochester. After two long days of tests and interviews, Dr. Levitt, awkward and stiffly formal in his suit and tie, invited Tucker and his father into his office.

"Emily is in excellent physical health," said Dr. Levitt, staring into the computer mounted on his desk. "Other than being profoundly autistic, of course."

"Autistic?" The Reverend raised his eyebrows. "Emily is not autistic."

The doctor looked at him, then back at the computer. "You didn't know she was autistic?"

Tucker said, "Isn't autism something you're born with?"

"That is correct," said the doctor, still staring into his screen.

"She didn't used to be like this," Tucker said. "Mom was happy. We used to do stuff, and talk all the time. Now she hardly talks at all. She just stays in the house and does her puzzles."

"She was perfectly normal," the Reverend said.

The doctor leaned closer to the screen. "Yes . . . I see you stated that in your admission papers, but people are often blind when it comes to loved ones. Your wife has been thoroughly examined by our specialists. She presents a classic autism-spectrum profile. Her social interaction skills are severely limited, her lack of affect is extreme, her repetitive behaviors and her anxiety when confronted with changes to her environment are a ninety-four-percent indicator for profound autism. . . . It *is* possible that she is suffering from RAD."

"What's RAD?" Tucker asked.

"Rapid-onset Autism-like Disorder. Quite rare, although we are seeing more cases in recent years, mostly in people who work in IT and other computer-related fields. Does your wife spend a lot of time online?"

"We don't even own a computer!" the Reverend said.

"In that case, I would suggest that although her symptoms may have recently become worse, they were always present. I very much doubt that it came upon her suddenly."

Tucker looked at his father, whose face was slowly turning red.

The doctor was rocking back and forth slightly as he stared into the computer screen. Oblivious, he continued speaking. "You must realize that autism is not a disease in the usual sense. It is not contagious, nor is it something that will go away—with or without treatment. Autism develops in the womb, perhaps even at conception." The doctor typed something into his computer. He pursed his lips. "She may be suffering from depression as well. We will need more tests. It is not always easy to diagnose psychiatric conditions in autistic patients."

"She. Is. Not. Autistic!" the Reverend said, his voice rising with each word.

The doctor sat back. "Mr. Feye, please control yourself."

"Control myself? My wife suddenly goes mad and you're telling me she was *born* that way? *Autistic?* What kind of doctor are you? You talk about her like she's a statistic, like she's not a person."

"I can assure you, Mr. Feye, I am well aware that Mrs. Feye is a person."

"How would you know? You're hardly a person yourself! Look at you, with your fish face and your starchy suit and your computer that you look at more than you look at us. My wife is not numbers on a screen!"

The doctor was turning red, too. "I'm afraid I must ask you to leave," he said.

"With pleasure." The Reverend stood up and stalked out of the room.

Tucker stood up slowly. "Is there anything we can do to make her better?" he asked.

"Find her another doctor," Dr. Levitt said stiffly. "Or better yet, another husband."

The ride home from Mayo was long and quiet. Tucker's mother sat in back, staring out the window, bobbing her head, counting mileposts.

"Are we going to see a different doctor?" Tucker asked as they passed milepost fifty-two.

His father, his mouth held in a hard straight line, shook his head.

One mile later, Emily Feye said, "Fifty-three."

Tucker said, "Maybe it would help to pray for her."

"Pray all you want," said the Reverend Feye after a very long pause.

"I will," said Tucker.

"Autism! The man is an idiot."

Tucker silently agreed.

"Fifty-four," said his mother.

"Do you know what I miss about God?" the Reverend asked.

Tucker shook his head.

"I miss having someone to blame things on."

"Fifty-five," said Emily Feye.

That night, Tucker prayed for his mother. He prayed for his father, too. The next morning—it was a Saturday—he found his mom in the kitchen cooking pancakes and sausages. She was fully dressed, and her hair was pulled back into a neat bun. The shades were up and sunlight filled the room. She looked at him and smiled in a way that made her look perfectly, happily normal.

"Morning, sleepyhead!" she said.

Tucker didn't know what to say. Had his prayers worked?

"You look good," he said, sitting down at the table.

She laughed and patted her hair. "I've really let myself go lately. You must have thought I'd gone completely out of my mind."

"So are you okay now?"

"I feel wonderful!"

"Where's Dad?"

"He went into church to work on the organ. How I miss playing that crazy machine! I feel like I've just woken up from a bad dream. The things that have been going through my head! Of course, I've always had quite an imagination. When I was little, I used to believe I was a princess. I lived in a magic castle with servants, who would bring me anything I wanted. Sometimes it seemed so real, I believed it was true."

"I guess little kids imagine a lot of stuff."

"I guess they do." She put a pancake and two sausage links on a plate and placed it before him. "Lately I've been remembering the strangest things. When I was a girl—I must have been six or seven—I remember walking home from school one day when two big black men came up the road."

"You mean like African Americans?"

"No, but they had black hair and black beards and they were wearing black suits. I thought they were Amish, so I wasn't afraid. One of them said something to me in a language I didn't understand, then the other one grabbed me and stuck something in my mouth, like a little plastic rod. A second later he yanked it out and they both ran off. I told my father, and the police went looking for the men but never found them. Later, Greta told me I must have imagined the whole thing." She shook her head, bemused by the memory. "But I don't know. . . . It was so real. . . ."

She prepared a plate for herself and sat down across from him.

"I'm sorry I've been acting so strangely, honey. I really don't know what came over me."

"That's okay," Tucker said. She'd had good mornings before. As he ate his pancakes, he allowed himself a glimmer of hope. Maybe this time it would last.

It didn't last.

They ate their breakfast, talking and laughing, just like old times. But after they were done eating, his mom retired to her chair in the living room and began working a sudoku puzzle. Soon she was staring into space and bobbing her head, her features slack, her eyes empty. Tucker looked at the puzzle in her lap. The blanks had been filled in with random numbers and made no sense whatsoever.

# 6 LIES

Tucker kept praying for his mother, but her good moments came less and less often. Most days she never changed out of her white cotton nightgown.

"I look like one of them," she said to Tucker one morning, staring at her blurry reflection in the polished steel side of the toaster.

"Them who?" Tucker asked.

"You don't see them?" She looked at him.

"See who?"

"Them." She pointed at the kitchen window. Tucker looked, half expecting to see someone staring in at them. "Ghosts," she said as she lowered the shade.

"There's no such thing," Tucker said, the hairs on the back of his neck stirring.

In fact, Tucker had seen two ghosts in recent weeks.

The first time, he had awakened early one morning and looked out his bedroom window to see a man made of fog staring in at him. For a fraction of a second, Tucker could pick out every detail of the man's features—a wide, down-turned mouth, a long nose, two close-set eyes, and a thick mop of colorless hair—then it was gone. It happened so quickly that Tucker didn't have time to be scared, and after a few minutes of perplexity, he decided that he must have imagined it.

The second ghost had appeared on the roof of the house in the middle of the day. Tucker had looked up and seen a faint, gaseous, humanlike shape standing on—or floating just above—the peak of the roof. The bright sunlight made it difficult to see any details, but Tucker had the impression that this time it was a woman, and that she was watching him. The image lasted for five or six seconds, slowly becoming harder to see, then it disappeared entirely.

Water vapor steaming from the hot shingles? A cloud of insects? Tucker had forcibly ejected both events from his mind and did not think about it again until his mother brought up the subject of ghosts.

"If there were really ghosts," Tucker said, "everybody would see them. Dad would see them too."

"He is one of them, Kosh."

"Kosh?" said Tucker.

His mother turned away as if he weren't present, opened the silverware drawer, and began polishing the clean spoons with the corner of her nightgown.

*   *   *

Tucker couldn't stop thinking about ghosts. His mom was getting more than weird; she was getting scary—calling him strange names and saying Dad was a ghost. He peeked through the half-open door of his dad's study. His father was sitting with his elbows propped on his desk next to a half-carved troll, his chin resting on his fists, staring bleakly into space.

Tucker pushed the door all the way open. "Dad?"

The Reverend closed his eyes. "Tuck."

"Mom says she sees ghosts."

The Reverend shook his head. "There are no such things as ghosts."

"I saw something on the roof."

His father's eyes snapped open.

"You stay off that roof," he said.

"I didn't say I was *on* the roof. I said I *saw* something there. Like a . . . like a ghost."

"A trick of the light. Heat distortion."

"It looked real."

"It *wasn't*," his father said with startling intensity.

Tucker decided to change the subject. "Mom counted her cornflakes this morning. She lined them up on the table and counted. She told me she was only hungry for thirty-nine flakes."

The Reverend did not reply.

"She's polishing the spoons again."

The Reverend's shoulders slumped.

"Maybe we should take her to another doctor," Tucker said.

"The doctors are useless."

"She called me Kosh."

Tucker's father turned and stared at him.

"Kosh?"

"Yeah. Who's Kosh?"

His father grimaced, as if the words caused him pain. "Nobody," he said.

"Are you okay?" Tucker asked.

"I'm fine," he said. "Why wouldn't I be?"

"I don't know," said Tucker. "You look sad."

"Happiness is overrated." The Reverend's expression softened. "I know this has been hard on you, Tuck. I'm sorry."

"I just want everything to be like before."

"Unfortunately, that's not how life works."

"How come you still preach, then?"

The Reverend's forehead knotted, but his mouth curved into a smile. "Because it's my job."

"But you don't believe in God."

"I believe in preaching." The Reverend swiveled his chair toward the window and did not say another word.

As his mother sank slowly into her private world of ghosts and clean light switches, as his father grew even more distant, as the crisp brown fields of autumn surrendered to a blanket of snow, Tucker distracted himself with school and snowmobiling with Tom and Will Krause. It had been five months since Lahlia had gone to live with the Beckers. He wondered whether she had learned to speak any English. He wanted to ask her how she had met his father. The Reverend Feye had steadfastly refused to talk about it.

Christmas came. The Reverend cut down a stunted spruce tree growing near the edge of the woods and dragged it home. His mother watched dully from her easy chair as Tucker and his father did their best to decorate the sorry little tree. It felt to Tucker as if they were faking it—just pretending to have Christmas. His dad bought him a snowboard, though, which gave Tucker another excuse to get out of the house as much as possible.

Emily Feye had become the subject of much gossip in Hopewell. Her increasingly odd appearance—white hair, staring eyes, quivering lips—was impossible to ignore. At home, she continued to cook and clean, but little more. One mid-January day, she left the house in her bathrobe and a long coat and walked into town. They got a call from Red Grauber, the owner of the Pigeon Drop Inn.

"Adrian, your wife is standing on the street in front of the old hotel talking to the air. You might want to come get her."

Tucker and his dad jumped in the car and drove downtown, where they found her huddled on the front steps of Hopewell House. She was happy to get into the warm car but seemed puzzled as to why they had come for her.

"I was just having a little walk," she said.

A few weeks later, on a cold Sunday in February, as the

Reverend was preaching on the care of the soul, Emily Feye stood up from her front-row pew and cried out, "I see them!"

The church went dead silent. She turned, facing the congregation. Her eyes lifted and she pointed at a space several feet above the heads of the parishioners.

"They watch us," she said. "Bugs in a bottle."

The Reverend, after a moment of stunned silence, said, "It is true. The souls of our departed loved ones watch us as they pave the way for us to one day enter the kingdom of Heaven. . . ." As he spoke, the Reverend stepped down from his pulpit and took his wife by the hand.

"I was a *princess,*" she said querulously.

Gently, he sat her down. She did not resist; the angry light faded from her eyes.

As the days and weeks and months passed, Emily Feye became even stranger and more ethereal. The Reverend now spent nearly every free hour in his study, reading or carving. Tucker felt as if both his parents were fading slowly away, growing more ghostly and insubstantial with each passing week.

# 7 THE SWING

By the time school let out in June, Tucker had almost gotten used to having a crazy mother and a depressed father. He spent his days fishing, exploring the patches of woods around Hopewell, riding the new mountain bike his dad gave him for his fourteenth birthday, and hanging out with the Krause brothers.

Tom and Will were good at coming up with exciting new ways to pass the time. Over the past year they had talked Tucker into several exploits, including capturing a young raccoon to keep as a pet, blowing up a can of gasoline, and jumping Thorp Creek with their father's snowmobile. The boys had survived all of these activities, sustaining only minor injuries: second-degree burns and a broken arm for Tom, rabies shots for Will, and a gash on Tucker's elbow requiring twelve stitches.

Tom's latest scheme was to build a rope swing. Not just any rope swing, but the mother of all rope swings. A few weeks earlier, while visiting their cousin Tony in Frontenac, Tom and Will had liberated a heavy-duty, hundred-foot-long rope from a barge that had run aground on the Mississippi. They hauled the rope back to Hopewell in their cousin's pickup truck. All they needed was a tree tall enough to do the rope justice. For this, they recruited Tucker, who knew the lakes and woods surrounding Hopewell better than he knew his own face.

Tucker took one look at the rope and grinned. He knew the perfect tree.

The next morning the boys cut up an old shipping pallet for steps. They piled the boards into a wheelbarrow, coiled the rope on top, and took turns pushing it up West End Road and through the Beckers' back soybean field to Hardy Lake.

A gigantic cottonwood rose from a steep bank at the south end of the lake. The trunk was six feet in diameter, and it was as tall as any tree in Hopewell County. They nailed the wooden steps to the trunk, making a crude ladder up to the lower crotch, where the tree forked into two heavy limbs. With one end of the rope tied to his belt, Tucker climbed up to the crotch, the rope growing heavier with each step. Wedging himself between the two limbs, he pulled up the rest of the rope hand over hand and draped it back and forth across the crotch.

He continued up the limb that arched out over the water. The rope played out slowly behind him.

Halfway up, several loops of rope slipped from the crotch. The sudden increase in weight nearly yanked him off the limb — but he managed to hang on. The Krause brothers watched from below, their mouths open.

Tucker continued shinning his way up the limb to a point where it forked into two smaller branches. He was over the lake now, the water sixty feet below him. The limb was only about six inches thick. Tucker was not usually afraid of heights, but he had never been *this* high before. His heart was banging so hard he could hear it in his ears. With his legs locked onto the branch, Tucker pulled the rope up to get more slack, then wrapped it several times around the fork and tied a triple knot. Just as he tightened the last loop, the remaining rope slipped from the crotch and flopped out over the lake, writhing and flailing. The branch jerked down as it took the full weight of the rope; Tucker clamped his body around the limb with all his strength as the branch bobbed and settled. The rope's contortions quickly dampened as its bottom end settled into the water about twenty feet from shore.

Briefly, Tucker considered climbing down the rope. That would really impress the Krauses. But he could not seem to make his legs release their grip on the tree. He closed his eyes, took a few calming breaths, wriggled carefully back down the limb to the main crotch, then descended the wooden steps to the ground.

Tom and Will were knee deep in the water, tying the bottom of the rope into an enormous knot. Once knotted, the end of the rope hung about two feet above the water. Tom added a thin nylon cord to the bottom of the knot. Will looked up at

Tucker, his face bright with excitement. He grabbed the end of the cord from his brother and scrambled up the bank, pulling the rope behind him. Tom followed.

"So, who goes first?" Will asked, looking down the steep bank to the water below.

Tom, looking up to where the rope was tied, said, "That branch looks pretty skinny."

"It's bigger than it looks," Tucker said. "And it held me."

"I weigh more than you." Tom was the oldest, tallest, and heaviest of the three, and the most cautious. He had not enjoyed the burns he'd received from the exploding gas can adventure or the broken arm from the snowmobile incident.

"I climbed up and tied it," said Tucker. "Somebody else should go first."

"Will's the smallest."

"Am not," said Will, even though it was clearly true.

"Maybe we should test it," said Tom. "Tie something heavy to it."

"If you think my knot's no good, climb up and check it," Tucker said.

"If you're so sure, *you* should be the one to test it."

"Maybe we should tie it around your neck and test it on *you*!" Tucker said.

"You scared?" Tom asked.

Tucker almost gave Tom a shove off the edge of the bank, but he managed to hold himself back.

"Okay," he said. "I tied it; I'll go first." He grabbed the

end of the nylon cord from Tom, but instead of jumping onto the big knot and swinging out from the top of the bank, he tied it to his belt, and climbed up the tree, dragging the rope behind him.

Will and Tom stared at him.

"Are you crazy?" Tom yelled.

"Yes," said Tucker. He climbed a few feet out on one of the branches. *I'm not that high up,* he told himself. He grasped the thick rope in his hands; it was a strong rope. He looked up at the knot he had tied, a good knot. He untied the leader cord from his belt and wrapped his legs around the rope, which hung in a steep arc, dropping for fifteen feet or so before beginning its journey back up to the branch high above him.

He waited, letting the urge to jump gather.

"You gonna do it or not?" Will yelled.

Tucker pushed himself off the branch—and went straight down. Time stretched. He opened his mouth in a silent scream, then felt the knot dig into the backs of his thighs as the rope went taut. The water rushed at him; the soles of his shoes skimmed the surface of the lake. Wind filled his open mouth; he rose into the blue sky, heading for the clouds.

At the top of the arc—a weightless moment that seemed to last far longer than it should have—he saw, hovering in the air before him, a transparent man. Impossible, but utterly real. He was close enough to see the individual strands of the man's swept-back hair, and the perfect teeth in his colorless smile.

Tucker nearly lost his hold on the rope, then he was swinging back, twisting his body to get a second look. His shoes touched the water again and he spun, the bank rushing past him, Tom shouting, and then a terrible, crushing force slammed hard into Tucker's back, and he was falling.

**8 MILKING THE SLAVES**

"Is he dead?" Will's voice.

"I don't know. He's not moving." That was Tom.

"What if he's dead?"

"He is not dead." A girl's voice, strangely accented.

"I think I saw his eyelid move," Tom said.

"What if he's paralyzed?" Will asked.

"He is not paralyzed," said the girl.

Tucker opened his eyes. Three faces framed by blue sky: Tom, Will, and a girl. Lahlia. Her hair was longer.

"You see?" she said. "He is alive."

Tucker drew a shuddering breath; a wave of pain rolled from his head to his feet.

"Are you okay?" Tom asked.

"It hurts."

"What if he broke his back?" Will asked.

"Move your legs," said Lahlia. "Show them."

Tucker moved his legs. He looked left and right. He was lying on the narrow strip of beach at the bottom of the bank, just a few feet from the water. Tucker pushed himself up into a sitting position. He felt as if he'd been run over by a combine.

"Did the rope break?" he asked.

"No, you idiot," Tom laughed. "You swung back and hit the tree trunk."

"Oh," Tucker said, looking at the towering cottonwood. "I didn't think of that." He climbed shakily to his feet.

"You rolled down the bank like a log," Will said. "Too bad we didn't get it on video. It would have been really cool."

Tucker tested each of his limbs. Everything seemed to work.

"How come you were twisting around like that?" Tom asked. "You were way up there and all of a sudden you started to spin."

"I thought I saw something," Tucker said. "Like a ghost."

"You saw a Klaatu," Lahlia said.

"A what?"

"A sort of ghost," said Lahlia.

"Does *Klaatu* mean 'ghost' in Bulgaria?" Tucker asked.

"What is Bulgaria?"

"Isn't that where you came from?"

"No."

"Then where *did* you come from?"

Lahlia thought for a moment, then shrugged. "I was raised in the Palace of the Pure Girls in the city of Romelas, where I was taken to the Cydonian Pyramid at the time of my Blood

Moon." Lahlia's dark eyes locked on Tucker. "Had you not appeared, the Lah Sept priests might have sent me through Gammel or Dal with a hole in my heart." She regarded Tucker with a slight tilt of her head and the hint of a smile.

"You must read a lot of fantasy books," Will said.

"This is why I do not talk about it," said Lahlia. "I knew you would not believe."

"Yeah, well, I don't believe in ghosts, either," Will said.

Tucker said, "Did you see it too? The ghost or whatever?"

Lahlia nodded. "Not everyone can see them. In Romelas they are considered bad luck."

"You didn't used to talk," Tucker said.

"I had nothing to say."

"You still got that little cat?"

Lahlia pointed. The gray cat was sitting at the top of the bank, cleaning its paws.

"His name is Bounce," she said.

"He hasn't grown much."

"Bounce is always the same."

"How come you don't go to school?" Will asked.

"Arnold says public schools breed sin and wickedness."

"That's weird," said Will.

Lahlia shrugged. "Arnold and Maria have many weird ideas. They enslave animals and draw milk from them. They consume animal flesh."

"You mean meat?" Tom said.

"Muscle tissue from mammals and birds."

"Everybody eats meat," said Will.

"Not everybody."

"Are you a vegetarian?"

"I don't consume animal products."

"No milk even? That's *really* weird," said Will.

As Lahlia talked with Tom and Will, Tucker watched. It was the only time he had ever been able to get a good look at her without her big black eyes staring back at him. He liked the way her upper lip lifted when she spoke. She was, he decided, kind of pretty.

"You find it strange because you are a primitive," she said to Will.

Will took a moment to consider that, then hopped around with a hunched back and bent legs, arms dangling, saying, "Hoo-hoo, ugh-ugh."

Lahlia frowned. "Are you in pain?"

"He's being a caveman," Tom said.

"Ork eat meat!"

"I once saw him eat seven hot dogs," Tom said.

Lahlia twisted her face. "It is bad enough to make animals into milk slaves, but grinding them up and stuffing them into their own intestines and then burning them over a fire is . . . barbaric."

"Ork barbarian! Ork throw girl in lake!" Will advanced upon Lahlia.

Instead of running away screaming as another girl might have, Lahlia stepped into Will's open arms. Her sharp shoulder connected with his belly, and in a graceful, apparently effortless motion, she lifted him into the air and *threw* him. Will landed in the shallow water with a tremendous splash.

Tom jumped back from the deluge. "Whoa!"

Will, sputtering and apparently uninjured, waded back to shore. "What happened?" he said.

"You just got your butt kicked by a girl," said Tom.

Lahlia was standing with her feet apart and her arms held out, her eyes locked on Will.

"I think she wants to do it again," Tom said.

"I wasn't gonna *do* anything," said Will.

"How'd you learn to do that?" Tom asked Lahlia.

"I have been trained to defend myself."

"No kidding!" Tom looked at his brother. "You okay?"

Will looked down at his dripping T-shirt and sodden jeans. "I am totally soaked."

"That what Ork get when Ork try to throw girl in lake," Tom said with a grin.

"I did not wish to get wet," Lahlia said, relaxing slightly.

Will peeled a glob of pond scum from his T-shirt and flung it into the water. "You could have just said so. Jeez!"

Tucker was feeling neglected—he had just smashed into a tree and could have died, and now the three of them were acting like he wasn't even there. He grabbed the rope and dragged it up the sandy bank.

"Where you going?" Tom asked.

"I'm going again," Tucker said.

"Are you nuts? You'll get killed."

"He will not die." Lahlia said, watching him.

Tucker tied the nylon cord to his belt and started up the tree, dragging the heavy rope behind him. Knowing that Lahlia was watching made him feel stronger and more confident. This time, he would show them what he could *really* do. He climbed out onto a limb ten feet higher than his previous launch site and edged his way out on the branch, as far as he dared. His new trajectory would take him away from the trunk. He hoped. Wedging the big knot between his legs, he looked down at the three tiny upturned faces, took a deep breath, and pushed off.

The ride was even better than before. He dropped twenty feet before the rope went tight, and the weightless moment at the end of the swing seemed to last twice as long. This time there was no ghostly face looking back at him. On the return swing he tensed himself for impact, but missed the trunk by several feet. He swung back and forth, looking up at leafy branches against the bright blue sky, until the rope slowed. Tucker jumped from the rope onto the shore.

Tom clapped him on the back. "All right!

Tucker, light-headed and proud, looked around for Lahlia.

She was standing at the top of the bank, holding Bounce, looking down at him. Beside her, wearing an amused smile, stood a man with long black hair tied back in a ponytail. He was dressed in faded black jeans and a leather vest decorated with silver studs.

"Nice one," he said to Tucker. He grinned and gave Lahlia a light punch on the shoulder. "Let's go, kiddo. Time to milk the slaves."

Lahlia moved away from him, not meeting his eyes. The man shrugged and walked off. Lahlia looked at Tucker. Her right hand twitched, the faintest of waves, before she turned and followed the black-haired man.

"Who was that?" Tucker asked.

"That," said Tom, "was Ronnie Becker."

# 9 THE LAST SUPPER

WHEN TUCKER GOT HOME LATE THAT AFTERNOON, HIS father emerged from his study and suggested that they catch some fish while his mom prepared dinner. Tucker was surprised and delighted — it had been a long time since he and his dad had done anything together. They dug some worms from the compost pile and walked down the path to the pond. Tucker told his dad about the rope swing, leaving out the part where he had crashed into the tree.

His father laughed when Tucker told about Lahlia throwing Will in the lake. Seeing his dad laugh — a wide smile breaking through the frown lines — Tucker felt joy, hope, and sadness all at once. It had been too long since they had laughed together.

"Do you remember the raccoon?" Tucker asked, bringing up one of their favorite family stories.

"How could I forget?" his father said.

One day, a couple of years ago, his mom had chased a young raccoon out of her vegetable garden. The raccoon panicked. Instead of running off into the woods, it ran through the open door into the house. The Reverend, hearing the commotion, came downstairs from his study to find a very frightened raccoon in the kitchen sink. After much screaming and shouting and broom swinging, the raccoon was herded out the door, where it ran straight between the thick legs of Mavis Setterholm, one of the church ladies, who had come by to drop off a fresh-baked rhubarb pie. Mavis screamed and fell backward onto her ample butt, throwing the pie in the air as she went down. The equally terrified raccoon hightailed it for the woods, and the pie landed upside down on Mavis's lap.

They had laughed about it for weeks.

"That raccoon, I bet he's the same one that's been upending our garbage can," the Reverend said as they stood side by side at the edge of the dock, watching their bobbers float. Thinking back to happier times, Tucker imagined that everything could be okay again. His father would regain his faith and his mother would be cured. That was what he had been praying for. Thinking to test this notion, Tucker looked from his red-and-white bobber to his father's craggy face.

"Remember when I was a little kid and I used to ask you why the sky was blue instead of green?"

"You always did have a lot of questions," his father said with a smile.

"You used to say it was because God made it that way."

The Reverend's face darkened. "The sky is blue because of the way atmospheric gases scatter sunlight, Tuck. This dock—"

He stomped his foot against the weathered planks. "I built this dock. God had nothing to do with it."

"Mom always says that when we make things, it's God working through our hands. I mean, she used to say that, before she got sick."

The elder Feye's eyelids stiffened; his mouth became smaller.

Tucker knew he should drop the subject, but sometimes his mouth talked on its own. "You used to say that too."

The Reverend stared at Tucker. After about two seconds, his eyelids relaxed.

"Your mother is an angel, Tuck." A deerfly landed on his forehead; the Reverend crushed it with the back of his hand. "But she is living in a world of her own."

"She still knows the names of things," Tucker said, staring at the smear of fly guts on his father's brow. "She still knows the names of all the flowers and trees."

The Reverend's smile became wistful. "She has retained that, at least."

"Maybe she really does see ghosts."

"Tuck, you know she is not right in her head. Watch your bobber!"

Tucker's bobber had disappeared beneath the surface of the lake. He jerked his rod up, felt a moment of resistance, then the bobber leaped out of the water, plopped back to the surface, and settled, sending out a succession of concentric, expanding ripples.

The Reverend grunted. "You lost him." He watched Tucker

reel in his line and lift the empty hook from the water. "Lost your worm, too." Another deerfly landed on the Reverend's arm and bit into him. He cursed and swung at it, but missed.

From behind them, a reedy voice filtered down through the maples.

"Your mother is calling us to dinner," said the Reverend. "Thank God. I'm getting eaten up out here."

They trudged up the path through the trees to the house, where Emily Feye stood on the porch waiting, hollow eyed, her forehead creased, her fine, brittle hair standing out—now almost completely white with faded orange at the tips. Her thin hands clutched at each other like fearful waifs.

Dinner was canned chicken soup, frozen broccoli boiled nearly to mush, and undercooked potatoes. Emily Feye's days as a formidable cook were far in the past. Still, Tucker would always remember that modest supper with his parents even though it was no different, really, from hundreds of others.

It would be their last meal together.

**10 FIREWORKS**

Tom and Will Krause showed up on their bikes shortly after dinner, just as Tucker was finishing the dishes.

"Rope swing!" Will yelled.

Tucker did not need a second invitation. He ran upstairs to tell his dad where he was going. He stopped short when he saw both his parents sitting on the edge of their bed. His mother was staring vacantly at nothing, her mouth open, her features slack. His dad sat close beside her, holding her hand. His cheeks were wet with tears.

"Dad?" Tucker had never seen his father cry—it frightened him.

"Tuck." The Reverend wiped his eyes with the back of his hand.

"Are you okay?"

The Reverend attempted a reassuring smile. "We're fine, Tuck."

Tucker did not know what to say. They weren't fine. Part of him wanted to throw himself on them and hug them both, while another part of him saw two strangers inhabiting his parents' bodies. The longer he stood there, the more uncomfortable he became.

"Was there something you wanted, Tuck?" his father asked, straining to hold on to his smile.

"Um . . . I'm going over to Hardy Lake with Tom and Will. . . . Is that okay?"

The Reverend nodded. His face relaxed, erasing the false smile.

"I'll be back soon," Tucker said.

"Take your time, son. Enjoy yourself with your friends."

That was a strange thing for his father to say. Usually he would say something like *Don't be late.* Or simply nod and say nothing at all.

"Are you sure everything's okay?" Tucker asked.

The Reverend said, "You know I would do anything for your mother. Anything."

"Me too," Tucker said.

"I know you would." His father tried to smile again, but failed. "Go on, Tuck. Your friends are waiting for you."

Tucker walked slowly back downstairs and outside. Tom and Will were already pedaling down the street. He hesitated. Maybe he should stay home. His dad seemed really upset. But what could he do? Nothing.

Tom and Will disappeared around the bend. Tucker felt a spark of anger. None of this was his fault. Why should he feel bad about going off with his friends? He looked back at the house. His mom and dad would still be there when he got home. It wasn't as if anything would change, as much as he wanted it to.

Tucker hopped on his bike and went tearing off down the road.

Tucker caught up with Tom and Will just as they reached Hardy Lake. Tom leaned his bike against the rope-swing tree, took off his backpack, and triumphantly dumped out an assortment of illegal fireworks: a brick of firecrackers, three Roman candles, and several packets of bottle rockets.

"Where'd you get 'em?" Tucker asked.

"Our cousin Tony," Will said. "He bought them in Wisconsin. Let's shoot some off!"

Tom said, "We gotta wait for dark."

"Yeah, right," Will said. "You just want to wait and see if Kathy Aamodt shows up."

"Shut *up*!" Tom said.

"Tom asked his girlfriend to come," Will said.

"She's not my girlfriend," Tom said.

"You got the hots for her."

"I do not. Anyway, she said she can't come."

Tucker believed Will, partly because just about

everybody had the hots for Kathy Aamodt, the best-looking girl at Hopewell Public, and in part because Tom was blushing.

Tom looked at the rope. "Who's first?"

They took turns, each time attempting to introduce a new variation into their routine. Tom did one swing standing on the knot. Will tried launching himself from farther out on the branch, which sent him spinning in a figure eight and brought him perilously close to the trunk. Tucker hung from the knot by his knees, holding the rope with one hand, letting the other hand skim the water as he arced low over the lake.

None of them had yet dared to let go at the high point—about thirty feet above the lake—and jump. Tucker had made several attempts, but at the critical instant, his hands had failed to unclench.

The other thing that prevented Tucker from letting go was the memory of the face he had seen the first time he had used the swing. Every time he reached the highest point of the arc, he half expected to see it again, but he never did.

As the sun dropped behind the trees, Will came up with a new variation. Tom was climbing the trunk for one more ride when Will unwrapped a packet of bottle rockets.

"What are you doing?" Tucker asked.

"Watch this." When Will Krause said "watch this," it often turned out to be interesting—and dangerous.

Tom settled himself on the branch and wrapped his legs around the rope.

"Are you gonna jump?" Tucker shouted.

Tom pushed himself off the branch with a howl—he always yelled as he dropped. The instant he left the branch, Will lit one of the rockets and held it out, pointing it over the lake. The rocket fizzed, then leaped from his hand, heading straight at Tom. It missed his feet by inches and exploded in a shower of yellow sparks.

"Hey!" Tom yelled on the backswing. "Cut it out!"

Will, laughing hysterically, lit a second rocket. This one zoomed right under Tom's butt. Tom dragged his feet hard in the water, slowing himself, jumped from the swing, and took off after Will.

Will dropped the matches and ran down the shore, laughing. Tucker was laughing too. A few seconds later he heard shouts, followed by a howl of pain. Soon, the brothers came walking back. Every few steps, Tom would slug Will in the shoulder, eliciting an angry curse with each blow.

Tucker knew that the best way to make peace between the two was to come up with something more interesting than fighting.

"C'mon, you guys, let's blow something up."

"Blow what up?" Tom said, once again hammering his knuckles into Will's shoulder.

"I saw some beer cans over there. We could pack, like, fifty firecrackers in a can and see if there's anything left after they go off."

"Forget it," Tom said. "Let's just go home. My shoes are soaked and I'm tired. Besides, the mosquitoes are coming out."

"Come on. It's just getting dark," Tucker said. "Tell you what: how about I swing and you guys try to shoot me?"

"You're crazy," said Tom. But Tucker could tell he was interested.

"You get two shots each. If you both miss, then one of you has to take a turn."

"What if we hit you?" Tom asked.

"Then I have to go again."

"Why build your swing on the edge of a lake if you are not going to jump?" The three of them looked up. Lahlia was standing on the bank, her face barely visible in the fading light. Bounce sat at her feet, his tail twitching.

"Why don't *you* jump?" Will said.

Lahlia did not deign to reply.

"Hey, you want to shoot a bottle rocket at Tucker?" Will asked.

"For what purpose?" she asked.

"It's a contest," said Tucker.

The doubtful look Lahlia was giving him made Tucker feel stupid and angry. He hated that look, and he hated anybody telling him what to do. He decided he had liked her better before she'd started talking.

Lahlia picked up her cat and climbed down the bank. "I heard explosions. I suspected it was you three doing something perilous." She nudged the bag full of fireworks with her foot. "Are these the noisemakers?"

"They're called fireworks," Tom said.

"How do they work?"

"You've never seen fireworks?"

Lahlia shook her head.

Tom lifted a handful of bottle rockets from the sack. "These are rockets," he said. "You light them here."

"And they make the noises?"

"I'll show you."

"Wait a sec," said Tucker, grabbing the rope. "Let me give you something to aim at." He pulled the rope up the bank and started up the tree trunk.

Will was all for it. "We can twist a bunch of rockets together," he said. "Light them all at once."

"Why does he want you to shoot rockets at him?" Lahlia asked Tom.

"He's crazy, I guess," said Tom.

Tucker crawled out along the branch as far as he dared. He wedged the rope between his legs. Funny thing—he wasn't scared at all. Excited, but not scared. Maybe a rocket would explode in his face and knock him out. Maybe he would fall into the lake and drown. He shrugged it off. Whatever happened would happen.

"You guys ready?"

"Hang on a sec," Will said. Tucker could see them fumbling with the rockets, twisting fuses together.

"Now?" He was ready to go and afraid if he waited any longer, he would lose the urge.

"Almost."

Tucker saw the flare of one match, then another.

"Okay," Tom shouted.

Tucker closed his eyes and pushed off. Time slowed. Each millisecond of his descent seemed to stretch. Images from the past year flickered through his head: the first time he saw Lahlia in her silver shift and blue stockings, his mother's frizzy white orange-tipped hair, his father's trolls, his father's tears. The rope went taut, the knot jammed into the backs of his thighs. He swung out, then up.

*This is it,* Tucker thought. He opened his hands and legs, and the rope left him. Cartwheeling through the dark, rockets whizzing past him filling the sky with yellow sparks and sharp, bright explosions, he imagined Lahlia's dark eyes upon him.

**11　NOBODY HOME**

It was nearly eleven when Tucker got home, an hour after his usual bedtime. The yard light, porch light, and the kitchen lights were all burning. Tucker leaned his bike against the garage and quietly let himself in through the side door. His parents were probably in bed, listening for his return. Or maybe they'd fallen asleep and wouldn't know what time he got in. He turned the lights off and crept up the stairs, staying to the outside of the treads to silence the creaks and squeaks. The house was remarkably quiet. His parents' bedroom door stood slightly ajar. Tucker peeked through the crack. Their bed was unoccupied and neatly made.

His dad was occasionally called away at night to minister to the sick or dying—but where could his mother have gone? He went downstairs and turned the lights back on. *Maybe they're out looking for me,* Tucker thought. If so, his dad would be furious when he got home. But why hadn't they left him a note?

Tucker looked outside. Their car was parked in front of the garage, so wherever they were, they hadn't driven there. Maybe they had walked over to their neighbors, the Reillys, or into town. Or someone had picked them up.

Tucker searched the rest of the house, feeling increasingly uneasy. He looked in the basement, checking the root cellar, the furnace room, and the workshop, opening each door with an increasing sense of dread. He ran back upstairs to his parents' bedroom and opened the door wide. Nothing. The bathroom looked reassuringly normal: three toothbrushes, his father's shaving mug and brush, his mother's fancy soaps and shampoos, the old-fashioned claw-foot bathtub. His father's study at the end of the hall contained the usual desk, chair, and books — but not his parents. He sat in his father's chair and thought. There were plenty of perfectly reasonable explanations, he told himself. One of his dad's parishioners might have driven over and said, *Help me, Reverend. My mother is dying and she needs you to pray with her!*

*Of course,* his father might have replied.

*Won't you come along, too, Mrs. Feye? My mother always liked you. . . .*

*Nah,* Tucker thought, *not likely.* Nobody in their right mind wanted anything to do with his mother, not these days. Another thought hit him: what if his mom had gotten sick, and his father had to take her to the hospital? No, the car was still here. Unless the car had failed to start. Maybe they'd called an ambulance. Maybe his father had had a heart attack. Tucker's brain reeled with morbid scenarios, none of which seemed likely when examined closely.

Whatever the explanation, the Reverend would not be pleased to find Tucker sitting in his study when he returned. Tucker turned off the light and closed the door behind him. He had looked everywhere—except in his own room. He pushed his bedroom door open and flipped on the light. Everything looked exactly as he had left it, except for a white envelope propped against his pillow. On the front, written in his father's strong, slanting hand, was his name.

Tucker opened the envelope. Inside was a single sheet of paper with a typewritten message.

```
Dear Tucker,
    Your mother has taken a turn for
the worse, and I am taking her to seek
treatment . . .
```

So they were at a hospital!

```
    . . . to a place where, unfortunately,
you will not be able to visit us.
    I don't know how long we will be
gone, so I have contacted your uncle
Curtis and asked him to take care of
```

```
you. You may expect him to arrive first
thing in the morning.
    Your mother and I wish you to
know that we love you very much. I am
confident that Curtis will care for you
to the best of his abilities.
```

At the bottom of the letter was his father's distinctive, angular signature, complete with the stylized cross at the bottom:

# PART TWO

# KOSH

*Although the diskos had become passé among her peers, Iyl Rayn continued to maintain her existing network, relocating only those disks that were too easily accessible to corporeals. Still, creatures of flesh and blood managed to find the diskos from time to time. She devoted herself to observing those who employed the portals, with particular attention to the diskos located in and around the geotemporal intersection once known as Hopewell County, Minnesota.*

— **E**³

 **12  OPTIONS**

Tucker awoke to the sound of thunder.

His mom would be upset. She hated storms. Then he remembered—his mother was gone. His father was gone.

He opened his eyes. Sunlight was pouring in through his bedroom window, but the thunder seemed to be getting louder. Tucker rolled out of bed and ran to the window. No clouds in sight. He could still hear the rumbling. A low-flying airplane, maybe? It was coming from the other side of the house.

The sound stopped abruptly—an engine shutting off. Tucker pulled on a pair of jeans and a T-shirt, ran downstairs, and opened the door.

A large, black, battered Harley-Davidson was parked between the garage and the house. Upon it sat a helmeted, leather-clad man of greater than average size. The man climbed off the bike and removed his helmet. His head was shaved. Thick black eyebrows crowded the center of his face. A prominent nose crooked to the right, as if he were trying to sniff his own cheek. His long chin bristled with several days' growth of black whiskers. His bright-blue eyes fixed upon Tucker and widened.

"I'll be damned," the man said.

Tucker did not doubt it.

"You Tucker?" the man asked.

Tucker nodded.

The man scowled. "You recognize me?"

Tucker shook his head. The man looked like a younger, beefier, outlaw version of Tucker's father, but he was sure he'd never seen him before.

"Are you Curtis?"

"Nobody's called me that in years. Call me Kosh."

*Kosh?* Tucker's mom had called *him* Kosh that one time.

"But you're my uncle Curtis, right?"

"That's right, kid. You sure you don't recognize me?" He walked toward Tucker, stopped about eight feet away, and peered at him closely. "I must be nuts. You look exactly like this kid I met one time." He took in the house, the garage, and the path down to the lake. "The old homestead. I remember it being bigger." He looked back at Tucker. "I suppose it's too much to hope that your old man came back and saved me the trouble of looking after you. I see his car's here."

"They didn't take the car," Tucker said. "I think they went to some hospital."

"That's what Adrian said." Kosh stepped closer, bringing

with him the smell of sweat, leather, and motorcycle. "They left last night?"

Tucker took half a step back. "They were gone when I got home. They left me a note."

"Can I see it?"

Tucker ran back inside to get the note. When he returned, Kosh was standing on the path looking out over the pond, his hands tucked in the back pockets of his black jeans. Tucker took the opportunity to check out the bike, an aging, battle-scarred Harley. Nearly every exterior surface was dinged, dented, crumpled, or scratched. The studded black leather seat was worn nearly through — it had been crudely patched more than once. The chrome plating had peeled away from the exhaust pipes, revealing rusting steel beneath. Tucker circled the bike, marveling that it had made it all the way to Hopewell. The license plate read KOSH5, implying at least four other Koshes — or, more likely, that this Kosh owned several other bikes.

Kosh came back up the path. Tucker handed him the note. Kosh read it, then held it out between his thumb and forefinger as if it were a dead mouse.

"That's it?"

"He left it on my pillow."

"Huh. Not even a God-bless-you." He released the letter and watched it fall to the ground.

"My dad doesn't believe in God."

Kosh raised an eyebrow. "Since when?"

"I don't know. A year, I guess."

Kosh laughed, shaking his head and slapping his dusty, greasy thigh to show Tucker how much he was enjoying the joke, whatever it was. Tucker felt himself getting angry.

"Do you know where they went?" Tucker asked.

Kosh stopped laughing but continued to shake his head. "They could be on the North Pole for all I know."

Tucker felt himself getting angrier. "I don't know why he'd want you to take care of me anyway. He doesn't even like you."

Kosh shrugged. "I never liked him much either, kid. But blood's blood. All I know is Adrian called and told me I'd be babysitting you for a while."

"I'm fourteen. I don't need a babysitter."

"Not saying you do. But here we are. Big brother has spoken." He gave Tucker a searching look. "So, Emily's not doing so good?"

"She sees ghosts." Tucker was instantly sorry he'd spoken, as if saying bad things about his mother would make it more true.

Kosh's lips tightened. "I don't know how she kept her marbles long as she did. Fifteen years with Adrian would drive anybody nuts."

"She's not *nuts*," Tucker said, louder than he meant to. "She's *sick*. The doctor said she has something like autism. He called it RAD. But Dad says the doctors don't know what they're talking about."

Kosh nodded somberly. "Yeah, Adrian told me they could

do nothing for her. He said he was going to try something else. Probably took her to some faith healer or witch doctor or something." He gave Tucker another long look, then put his hands on his hips and turned toward the house. "Guess we better get busy shutting this place down."

"What?"

"Turn off the water, shut off the electricity —"

"Wait — how come?"

"We can't just leave it, kid."

"Leave? Who's leaving?"

"You and me, kid. You're coming to live with me."

"I'm not going anywhere with you." Tucker ran up the porch steps and into the house.

"If you think I'm staying here in Hopeless, you're crazier than your old man," Kosh said.

Tucker slammed the door and locked it, his heart hammering. He could hear Kosh just outside, muttering curses. Maybe he would give up and go away. But then what? He could go to live with the Krauses. Or maybe just stay at home and hope that his parents' absence would go unnoticed. He could make up a story, tell everybody that they had gone to visit a sick relative, and wouldn't be back for a few weeks. That would buy him some time. Or he could live in the abandoned Hopewell House, like the Phantom of the Opera. He had sneaked into the abandoned hotel once with Tom and Will. Some of the rooms still had beds, dusty but serviceable. When one room got dirty, he could simply move down the hall. Tom and Will would bring him food, and what they couldn't get for him he would steal.

He was wondering how he would stay warm come winter when Kosh banged on the door.

"Open up, kid. I know you can hear me."

Tucker imagined Kosh smashing his fist right through the wood panel.

"C'mon, kid, I just want to talk."

"My name isn't *kid*," Tucker yelled at the door.

"Okay, then. Tuck. Open the door, Tuck."

"It's *Tucker*." Only his father called him Tuck.

"Tucker, then. Would you please open the door so we can discuss this?"

"I'm not leaving."

"Okay, okay! I won't make you go if you don't want to."

"How do I know you're telling the truth?"

"You don't. But I am." In a softer tone, he said, "Look, I just rode two hours to get here. You could at least offer me something to drink."

If Kosh wanted to, he could probably knock the door right off its hinges, Tucker thought. His parents wouldn't like that. He unlocked the door, opened it, and backed away. Kosh stepped inside.

"Thanks." He walked past Tucker into the kitchen, and opened the refrigerator. "No brewskis?"

"My parents don't drink," said Tucker.

"Look at all this food. What are we going to do with it?"

"Eat it," Tucker said.

"Oh, right. I forgot. You aren't leaving." He found a bottle of apple juice, sat down at the kitchen table, and drained it in one long swallow. "You know what'll happen if you stay here, don't you?"

"I'll be fine."

"Yeah, but for how long?" Kosh said. "Let me tell you what'll happen. You'll be fine for a few days. Eating whatever you want, staying out half the night with your friends, raising all sorts of hell, trashing the place. Maybe you got some cash, and you can stretch it out a few weeks. Maybe you even take the old man's car for a spin, maybe roll it over in a ditch, bust your schnoz on the steering wheel." Kosh put a finger to the side of his misshapen nose. "Or maybe some other stuff happens. Either way, sooner or later some nosy neighbor will come poking around and find out you been living the high life all on your lonesome. Next thing you know you're stuck in a foster home with the Do-Good family. Or more likely, they send you to a state school. You ever been in a state school?"

Tucker shook his head.

"It's like being in prison, kid. Turn you into a criminal if you aren't one already. Assuming you survive."

Tucker felt disconnected from reality, as if Kosh were nothing but a hologram of a real person. But what he was describing sounded all too real.

"You're in a vise, Tucker. I feel for you, I really do. Fact is, you just don't have a whole lot of options. We got a common agenda here. You don't want nothing to do with me, and I sure as hell want nothing to do with you. I barely survived the last time we met."

"But . . . we've never met."

"Maybe not." Kosh narrowed his eyes. "You just look awful familiar. Sometimes I think crazy runs in the family. You aren't crazy, are you?"

"No. I have a plan." Tucker thought about his scheme to become the Phantom of Hopewell House. But even as he thought it, the idea unraveled. People would notice lights at night, they would hear him moving around, and he would be caught in no time. And he didn't have much money, not even enough to buy a bus ticket out of town.

"You're a smart kid — I can tell. But life's got a way of taking the best plan and whacking you upside the head with it. Look at me. I was planning to paint the south side of my barn today. Then I get a call from my dear brother and next thing I know, I'm sitting in a kitchen in Hopeless, Minnesota, drinking apple juice instead of beer and talking to a twelve-year-old kid —"

"I'm fourteen," Tucker said.

Kosh grinned, and suddenly he looked like a completely different person. "Well, I'm thirty-two, and what do I know? Look, you come stay at my place, you'll do fine. You get your own room. And when your folks come back, they'll know right where to find you."

The more Kosh talked, the less scary he became. Tucker even started to imagine himself on the back of that monster Harley.

"Would you teach me to ride?"

Kosh tipped his head. "I got a little Honda dirt bike might fit you."

Tucker thought for a few seconds. "People are going to wonder where we went."

"Adrian took care of that," Kosh said. "Said he let enough people know so they won't think I kidnapped you."

"What about all my stuff?"

"There's not much room in my saddlebags," Kosh said. "How much stuff are we talking?"

"We could take my dad's car. Load the food from the fridge and all my clothes and stuff."

"What about my bike?"

"You could put the bike on the trailer." Tucker pointed at the utility trailer parked alongside the garage.

Kosh thought for a moment, then sighed. "Okay, kid, we'll do it your way."

"It's *Tucker*."

Kosh rolled his eyes. "Tucker."

## 13 THE DISK

KOSH'S HARLEY FILLED MOST OF THE TRAILER, BUT there was room for Tucker's bicycle, the perishable food, a couple of suitcases, and a few other items: his chess and checkers set, an old microscope that sort of worked, a poster showing the New York City skyline, his old metal fire truck, his snowboard—

"Why are you bringing *that*?" Kosh asked.

"It's mine," said Tucker.

"It won't snow for another six months. You'll probably be home before school starts. Your folks won't be gone forever."

Tucker's insides went hollow as he looked at the snowboard, the only gift he had received on that last sad, lonely Christmas. The stunted spruce tree he and his dad had decorated was now rotting in the brush pile behind the garage. Was it true that his parents would be back before the end of summer? He was not so sure.

Kosh said, "Look, anything we leave behind, you absolutely got to have it, we can come back. My place is only a couple hours away. Okay?"

What Kosh said made sense, but that didn't make it any easier. If he could, Tucker would have strapped the entire house to the top of the car.

"Let's lock and load and hit the road," Kosh said.

Tucker put the snowboard back in the garage. He was trudging toward the car when he noticed the aluminum extension ladder leaning against the back of the house. It wasn't like his dad to leave things out, so why was the ladder there? He thought back to the day his dad had disappeared off the roof.

"You coming or not?" Kosh said.

"Just a minute." Tucker ran to the ladder and started to climb.

"Hey, where you going?" Kosh yelled.

Tucker ignored him. He stepped from the ladder onto the steep roof. Only the grip of his sneaker soles on the rough asphalt shingles kept him from sliding off. He quickly reached the peak, grabbed on to the chimney, and looked around. He could see the repair his father had made last year. The replacement shingles were a slightly different color from the originals. He looked up the road, but no one was in sight. In the distance he could see the Hopewell water tower, the roof of Hopewell House, and the radio tower.

"Tucker, come on down." Kosh had climbed to the top of the ladder.

There was something very strange about that roof. It was where his father had disappeared the first time and where Tucker had seen one of the ghosts. He scanned the horizon, looking from downtown Hopewell to the Reillys' silos on the far side of the pond. The water was choppy. A light breeze ruffled his hair. He turned his head and looked east, toward the woods. Tucker blinked and rubbed his eyes. The trees seemed to waver. It didn't change anything. Something just off the end of the roof was blurring a section of horizon. "There's something up here," he said over his shoulder.

"Kid . . . come on!"

Tucker got down on his hands and knees and crawled along the ridge toward the edge. If he didn't look at it directly, he could make out a perfectly round distortion of the air—a gauzy cloud had been compressed into the shape of a four-foot-diameter disk—but the closer he got, the harder it was to see. He heard a faint humming sound, like a swarm of tiny insects. He smelled something like burning oil, and he felt a tugging sensation, as if the disk were sucking at the fabric of his shirt. He was reaching out his hand when something grabbed his belt and yanked him back.

"What do you think you're doing?" Kosh shouted in his ear.

"Do you see that?" Tucker pointed, but there was nothing to point at. The disk was gone. He could no longer hear the faint hum; the air was perfectly clear.

"See what?"

"There was something there," Tucker said.

"Yeah, well, if there was, it's gone. Now come on. You almost fell off the roof. I don't want you breaking your scrawny neck on my watch."

Neither Tucker nor Kosh talked as they followed the county road out of town toward I-90. The trees and buildings and signs became less familiar with each passing mile. Kosh turned onto the freeway and brought the Chevrolet up to seventy miles per hour as Tucker stared numbly out through the windshield. He felt as if he was living in a dream, as if he might wake up and the entire last year would go away. Maybe he *was* crazy. Seeing ghosts. The thing on the roof. His dad disappearing. Lahlia, with her strange ways and even stranger stories.

After a few more miles, Kosh spoke.

"You thought you saw something up on the roof, huh?"

Tucker turned his head slowly to regard the man behind the wheel.

"I *did* see something."

"Not saying you didn't."

"I could smell it. And hear it."

Kosh drove for a while without replying. Finally, he spoke.

"Life really sucks sometimes."

Tucker laughed. "Yeah, right. And then you die."

"That's right, kid."

"*Tucker.*"

"Yeah. Tucker," Kosh said with a smile.

## 14    THE BLACK BARN

Kosh Feye lived on an old farmstead north of La Crosse, Wisconsin, in a black barn.

"You live in a *barn*?" Tucker said.

"House burned down ten years ago," Kosh said, pointing to a collapsed, charred foundation with ragweed and nettles growing up through the rubble.

"You painted your barn *black*?"

"I like black." Kosh lifted one of Tucker's boxes from the trunk.

"What's *that*?" Tucker pointed at the top of the barn, where the dark profile of a motorcyclist stood on a short post.

"Weather vane," said Kosh. "He always rides against the wind. Made it myself. Come on, I'll show you your room."

The bottom level of the barn was a sprawling garage/workshop/junkyard containing several motorcycles, an ATV, two tractors, a snowmobile, and a school bus with no wheels.

"You got everything," Tucker said. "Except a car."

"Don't like cars," said Kosh. "Anyway, we got Adrian's Chevy now." A long worktable was covered with engine parts. More machine parts and tools were stacked on metal shelves and hanging from hooks on the walls. They threaded their way through the shop to a black iron spiral staircase. Tucker followed Kosh up the steps through the ceiling.

The second floor was a different world: a single open space the length of the barn, with polished wooden floors and a bank of picture windows looking out over a forested valley. An enormous stone fireplace dominated one end of the room. At the other end was a kitchen area with a wall of stainless-steel appliances. A black leather sofa and chair were positioned in front of the fireplace; a wooden trestle table and chairs divided the kitchen from the rest of the room. The center of the space, an area about fifty feet long, was open and empty.

"You could have a bowling alley here," Tucker said.

"I don't bowl."

"You got a computer?" Tucker asked.

"Nope."

"My dad never wanted one either."

"Probably the only thing me and your old man got in common," said Kosh.

"TV?"

"Sorry," Kosh said, not sounding in the least bit sorry.

Tucker walked to the windows and looked out over the valley.

"Nice view," he said.

"This way," said Kosh.

The spiral staircase continued up through the second-floor ceiling. The third floor was unfinished. It had the musty, sour smell of old wood, new wood, and gypsum dust. One end was full of stacked two-by-fours, drywall, and plywood. Barn swallows sailed in and out the open windows at the peaks. Bits of rotting straw were scattered across a rough wooden floor. The other end of the space was framed in with two-by-fours and sheets of drywall.

"Under construction," Kosh said. "Your room's over here."

Tucker followed him through an open doorway into the maze of studs and unfinished walls. Kosh led him down a short hallway to a corner room that was nearly finished. A futon mattress lay on the carpeted floor, along with a small chest of drawers, a desk, a chair, and a crookneck reading lamp. A large window looked out over the valley.

Kosh dropped the suitcases on the floor. "No AC, but you got plenty of ventilation."

"Where do *you* sleep?"

"Wherever I happen to be when I get tired. Cot in the workshop, sofa, wherever. I don't sleep much."

"I'm not taking over your bedroom, am I?"

Kosh snorted. "I'm not *that* nice of a guy."

Except for the frequent sputters and roars from gasoline engines, life in the black barn was peaceful . . . and a little boring. Tucker could do what he wanted, as long as he cleaned up his own messes.

For the first few days, Tucker explored Kosh's property and the surrounding woods and tried to avoid thinking about his parents or about Hopewell. But every time he stopped moving, his thoughts turned to home, to life as it had been, long ago, before everything changed. His father standing in his pulpit at church, preaching with God's light in his eyes. His mother in the garden, her red hair tied back, a hoe in her hands, smiling and joking with him. He wondered if he would ever see them that way again — or see them again at all.

It was too hard to think about. Even his more recent memories — Tom and Will, the rope swing, Lahlia — left him feeling hollow and lost. Especially Lahlia, who kept popping into his thoughts: holding the gray kitten, looking down at him when he'd fallen from the rope swing. Lahlia as she had appeared that day with his father, wide eyed and mute in her tattered silver shift and blue plastic booties, staring at him with those dark eyes.

Tucker wondered if Kosh was haunted by memories, too — maybe that was why he worked so hard. He never stopped doing stuff. His various projects included engine repair, mowing his field, working in his vegetable garden, putting a fresh coat of black paint on the barn with his power sprayer, remodeling the third floor, and cooking. Kosh worked as hard on his cooking skills as he did on all his other projects. One night it was lamb chops with wild rice, sweet corn and zucchini from the garden, and a salad of watercress gathered from the creek that ran through the property. The next day Kosh made individual chicken potpies and roasted potatoes, along with a salad composed from baby lettuce plants and nasturtium blossoms from his garden. Tucker watched the scowling, leather-clad biker arranging the blossoms on a china salad plate with his thick, permanently grease-stained fingers. It was like watching a gorilla assemble a watch.

"How did you learn to cook?" he asked.

"I used to cook for Adrian and me. And I worked at the Drop for a while."

"The Drop? You mean the Pigeon Drop Inn?"

"Yeah. Flipping burgers." He carefully placed a few raspberries around the rims of the salad plates and set them on the table. "'Course, nobody ever got food like this at the Drop."

"How come you left Hopewell?"

"You kidding me? Why would anybody stay in Hopeless?"

"What were you like when you were my age?" Tucker asked.

Kosh thought for a moment. "I had a minibike. Later on I had a dirt bike. I mostly hung out with Ronnie Becker and some other kids."

"What was my dad like?"

"When I was your age? Adrian must've been about twenty-four. Had his nose in a Bible most of the time."

"So he was always religious?"

"Pretty much, especially after our dad died."

"Was Mom his girlfriend then?"

"That came later."

"Were you, like, a juvenile delinquent?"

"I got in my share of trouble. Why? You considering that as a career path?"

"I heard Ronnie Becker got caught growing marijuana behind their barn. Were you guys, like, drug dealers?"

Kosh laughed. "Ronnie was growing ditch weed and selling it to college students in Mankato. I had nothing to do with it."

"Did anything weird happen when you lived in Hopewell?"

"Weird like what?"

"I don't know. Weird." He was thinking about the disk, and the ghosts.

"There was this one time. . . . I was seventeen." Kosh put the salads on the table. "I was downtown when I heard this banging noise coming from the old boarded-up hotel, and all of a sudden this guy kicks his way out, right through the front door. Somehow he'd gotten stuck inside. He comes stumbling out onto the street, a big bearded guy dressed in a long black wool coat and a black hat even though it was about ninety degrees out, and he was talking really fast in some language I'd never heard before. I figured he was drunk. He runs right up to me and starts tugging at his beard and yelling gibberish, and I was like, *Huh?* Then he throws up his hands and takes off running down the road."

"Then what happened?"

"He just ran off. I figured from the hat and coat that he was

Amish or something, or maybe one of those Jews like they have in New York that dress like the Amish. Except the Friedmans were the only Jews in Hopewell, and they dressed just like everybody else, and the nearest Amish people lived way over in Harmony. Either way, nobody could figure out what the guy was doing in Hopewell, or how he'd got in the hotel."

"What happened to him?"

"Chuck Beamon said he saw him running across his soybean field being chased by a pig, but you couldn't trust anything Chuck said. As far as I know, nobody ever saw him again." He looked at Tucker. "That weird enough for you?"

"Mom told me she was once grabbed by a couple of guys dressed in black. They stuck something in her mouth, then ran off."

Kosh nodded. "She told me about that. She said it was a dream."

"What was it like when your dad died?"

Kosh didn't speak for a very long time, then he said, "I was ten. It was bad."

"What was he like?"

"He was . . . well, he was my *dad*. What can you say about your dad at that age? He was the center of the universe. After he was gone . . . it was like somebody tore the heart right out of me."

Tucker didn't know what to say to that. Kosh put the potpies on the table. They sat down. Kosh picked at his salad. Tucker tasted one of the nasturtium blossoms. Peppery.

"I heard you ran off with Ronnie Becker," he said.

"We took off about the same time, if that's what you mean. Hung out for a while, then went our separate ways."

"Did you and Dad have some kind of fight?"

Kosh's mouth tightened. "It was a long time ago. Let it go. I did." He pointed his fork at Tucker's plate. "Shut up and eat."

Tucker dug into his potpie. It was delicious. He set down his fork.

"What's the matter? You don't like it?" Kosh said.

Tucker's eyes were burning; he set his jaw, willing himself not to cry.

"It tastes just like my mom's," he said.

Kosh looked away. Tucker picked up his fork.

Kosh said, "Yeah, well, it ought to—she taught me how to make them." He cleared his throat. "Emily was always a good cook."

## 15 EYEBROWS

The next morning, Tucker reminded Kosh of a promise he had made back in Hopewell.

"I said *what*?" Kosh raised his eyebrows.

"You said you had a dirt bike I could ride."

"And you're, what, like, ten years old?"

"You know how old I am."

"Hmm . . ." Kosh put a hand to his chin and stared, hard and long, at his nephew. Tucker stared back, silently daring him to go back on his word.

An hour later, Tucker was racing full throttle down the driveway on a 125cc Honda with Kosh shouting after him to slow down. Slow down? What fun was that? Tucker throttled back, figuring that if he didn't, Kosh might never let him ride again. He made a cautious U-turn where the driveway met the highway and rode back at a more sedate pace.

Kosh stood with his arms crossed. "You got that out of your system?"

Tucker nodded, grinning.

Kosh snorted. "Like hell you do. Lesson over."

"I'll be careful!"

"You can be careful tomorrow. We got a storm coming in." As if on cue, large raindrops began to fall. "Let's see if you can put that thing away without busting anything."

They reached the barn just as the rain began in earnest. Kosh went to one of his benches and immediately went to work rebuilding a 1967 Triumph carburetor. With nothing else to do, Tucker sat on a stool and watched his uncle hand-cutting gaskets, filing invisible burrs, and swearing creatively and lengthily every time he dropped a screw, which was often. Aside from learning a few combinations of cuss words that otherwise might never have occurred to him, Tucker was bored.

"How come you don't work?" Tucker asked.

"What does it look like I'm doing?"

"I mean at a job. Don't you need money?"

"I sell a bike now and then."

"How did you afford to buy this place?"

Kosh looked up from his work. "After the old man died, Adrian and I sold his barbershop to Janky, so we had a little money put aside. Eventually, Adrian got married and used his share to buy himself a pipe organ and a church. I bought this place."

"He never talks about you much."

"I don't talk much about him, either."

"Yeah, but—"

"Look, why don't you go do something useful?"

"It's raining."

"It does that sometimes."

"Were you ever in jail?"

Kosh set his jaw and fed a tiny screw into a countersunk hole. Using a fine-tip screwdriver—in his big hands it looked like a toothpick—he carefully tightened the screw. He did not reply to Tucker's question.

"How come you're not married?" Tucker asked.

"Not your business."

"You got a girlfriend?"

"Nope."

"Did you ever?"

Kosh stabbed the screwdriver into the wooden workbench and gave Tucker a glare intended to be stern and scary. "Kid, if you don't stop with the questions I'll stuff an oil rag in your mouth."

Tucker grinned. "Was Ronnie Becker like, your boyfriend?"

Kosh threw up his hands. "I know what this is. You've been sent by Satan to give me a preview of hell."

"Do you believe in God?"

"I believe in the devil, that's for damned sure—I got you to prove it." He shook his fist at the ceiling. "Adrian, this is all your fault, you self-righteous Bible thumper!"

This was much more interesting than watching him rebuild a carburetor, Tucker thought.

"How come you're working on the Triumph carburetor, anyways?" Tucker said. "You never ride it."

"I don't ride it because it's got a bad carbur—" Kosh stopped mid-word and shook his head violently.

"I'm hungry," Tucker said.

"Go make yourself something."

Tucker figured he'd pushed Kosh as far as he could, and besides, he *was* hungry. He climbed the stairway to the second floor and looked through the cupboards and refrigerator for something to eat. The problem was that Kosh didn't have anything like cereal or peanut butter. He cooked everything from scratch. The simplest thing Tucker could think of was scrambled eggs. He had watched his mom make them. It looked easy. Just beat some eggs, throw them in a pan, and stir it around a bit. Everything went according to plan right up to the point where the kitchen towel caught on fire. While Tucker was beating out the towel, he managed to upend the pan, covering the stove burners with uncooked egg. He cleaned up as best he could, although he had a little trouble getting the gas burners put back together the right way.

Kosh came upstairs just as Tucker finished putting the stove back together.

"What did you burn?" he asked.

"I was trying to make scrambled eggs and the towel caught on fire."

"All by itself?"

"Um . . . I might have put it on the stove." Tucker wasn't sure what to expect.

Kosh considered his nephew. "You still want eggs?"

Tucker nodded.

"I'll show you how to make scrambled eggs." Kosh put a sauté pan on the stove. "First, you use a pan, not a towel." He turned on the burner. Nothing happened. He removed the pan and twisted the knob back and forth. He leaned close over the burner, trying to see what was wrong with it.

"This doesn't look right," he said.

In answer, a plume of sooty orange flame erupted from the stove and sent him staggering back with a howl.

"What the hell did you do to my stove!" he yelled. Kosh appeared to be undamaged—except for his eyebrows, which had turned into curly white caterpillars.

"Your eyebrows," Tucker said.

"What *about* them?" Kosh dragged his arm across his forehead. The singed eyebrow hairs disintegrated into ash.

The loss of his eyebrows made Kosh understandably grumpy. His mood was not improved by Tucker's apologies. Tucker hovered nearby, offering to help as Kosh set about repairing the stove.

"Do you need me to get any tools?"

"No."

"Do you want me to hold that?"

"No."

"Can I—?"

Kosh turned to him and scowled. "Listen, kid, I want you nowhere near this stove. The best thing you can do is make yourself scarce." With two pale bald spots where his eyebrows used to be, Kosh was not his usual fearsome-looking self. Tucker bit his tongue, trying not to laugh, but could not hold back a smile.

"Something funny?" Kosh asked.

"Nope," said Tucker.

"Go do something."

"Do what?"

"It's not raining anymore. Go ride your bike around the field."

Tucker was more than happy to comply. He ran downstairs and started the bike, and rode out of the barn. The driveway was slick and muddy—he almost dumped the bike in the first ten seconds. He rode carefully out to the field and around the perimeter, but the grass was wet and slippery, and he couldn't go very fast. He rode back to the driveway, then out to the road. He stopped next to the mailbox and glanced back at the barn. He felt guilty about messing up Kosh's stove, but he was also a bit angry. It wasn't his fault. He hadn't asked to come live here, and he hadn't broken the stove on purpose. He looked at the road. The asphalt surface was mostly dry. It would be nicer to ride on than the muddy field. Kosh would be busy with the stove for a while, and cops were few and far between in Trempealeau County. He revved the bike and pulled out onto the road. It felt great—smooth, dry, and solid. Tucker accelerated, leaning hard into the curves. The feeling of freedom and weightlessness reminded him of the rope swing.

Each twist in the road came on a little faster. He loved how the tires clung to the pavement. As he headed into a particularly sharp curve, his rear wheel hit a patch of gravel. Tucker fought for control, the rear of the bike slewing back and forth. The rear wheel caught and sent Tucker flying off the bike into a patch of tall weeds. He rolled several yards through a soft mass of vegetation before coming to rest. His first thought was that he was very lucky to be alive. His second thought was that he had been attacked by ten million mosquitoes. The weed patch was solid nettles. His arms, his legs, his face—everything—itched like no itch he had ever experienced. He had landed so hard that the nettles stung him right through his T-shirt. He dragged himself out of the weeds, skin shrieking. After a few seconds of clawing at himself, Tucker realized that he was only making it worse. He forced his arms to stop moving and climbed out of the ditch to the road.

His motorcycle was nowhere in sight. Tucker walked along the side of the road, peering into the dense woods, trying to not think about his prickling skin. Fifty yards away, he found the twisted ruin of the dirt bike wrapped around the trunk of a maple.

Kosh would not be happy.

He walked the three miles back to the barn, trying to come up with a good story. He failed. By the time he reached the driveway he had blisters on his heels, his neck was sunburned, and he still itched everywhere. As he walked up to the barn, something caught his eye just above the peak of the barn near the motorcycle weather vane. A wavering of the air like he had seen over their house in Hopewell. He moved toward the barn, keeping his eyes on the spot, waiting for it to move, or disappear. As he shifted to the side he could make out the shape of a disk.

Could it be heat rising off the barn roof, somehow reflected by the shingles? He didn't think so. It was something else, something unearthly.

"Where have you been?" Kosh was standing in the doorway with his arms crossed.

Tucker pointed to the top of the barn.

Kosh stepped outside and looked up. "What?"

"Can't you see . . . ?" Tucker stopped talking. The disk was gone. "I thought I saw something up there. Like a disk."

Kosh shook his head slowly. "There's nothing there," he said.

"I saw—"

"Maybe you saw a cloud of gnats. Now tell me how you got all scratched up."

# 16  ON THE ROOF

"I swear you must have a death wish," Kosh said as he smeared a paste of baking soda and water on Tucker's arms. "The only reason I don't hang you up by your toes and beat you is because I used to be twice as dumb."

"What was the dumbest thing you ever did?"

"Invited you to come live with me."

"Oh." Tucker thought his uncle was kidding, but he wasn't sure enough to press the matter.

"I'm really sorry," Tucker said.

"Me too, kid. That was a nice little bike."

"I mean about everything. Coming to live here, and the stove, and . . . everything."

"How's that feel?"

"Being sorry?"

"No. The itching. You want some of this goop on your neck?"

"That's okay. It doesn't itch so bad anymore."

Kosh stood up and wiped off his hands. "You don't have to feel sorry about staying here," he said. "I don't mind so much."

For the next few days, Tucker kept a low profile and managed not to wreck anything. He checked the roof of the barn several times a day, but the disk did not reappear. Kosh's eyebrows began to grow back—they looked like gray smudges. Every time Tucker looked at him, he had to suppress a laugh.

One morning, as they were eating pancakes for breakfast, Kosh sat back in his chair and regarded Tucker.

"What?" Tucker said.

"You think if I leave you on your own today, you can try not to kill yourself?"

"Where are you going?"

"I got to ride up to Whitehall and pick up a license, then up to Eau Claire for some parts."

"Can I come?" Tucker asked.

"No. I'll be gone most of the day. During that time, you will not lay a hand on any tool or any piece of machinery, including my stove and my remaining motorcycles. Do not enter my workshop for any reason. Furthermore, do not run, climb, ride, kick, slide, throw, pry, hammer, or in any other way risk damage to yourself or, especially, any of my property. Do you understand?"

Kosh's missing eyebrows were no longer quite so amusing.

"So what am I supposed to do?"

"Sleep. Read. Contemplate the universe."

"Just sit here all day and do nothing?"

"That would be ideal," said Kosh.

A few minutes later, sitting on his bed doing absolutely nothing, Tucker heard Kosh ride off. As the sound of the Harley faded into silence, a sense of loneliness and gloom settled upon him, soon to be replaced by irritation at Kosh, who seemed bent on eliminating his every source of entertainment. Doing nothing was *hard*. Tucker lay back on his bed and tried to read a book, but the words skittered back and forth on the page. If he didn't get up and *do* something he would go crazy. He threw the book aside and went outside. He could poke around in the woods. He could weed the garden. He could walk to the end of the driveway and check the mailbox. None of those options seemed interesting. He looked up at the weather vane on top of the barn.

He blinked and rubbed his eyes, then looked again.

The disk had returned.

Climbing onto the barn roof certainly qualified for Kosh's list of forbidden activities . . . but it wouldn't hurt to take a look. There were ladder rungs nailed to the south wall of the barn. Tucker had never climbed them, but he'd checked them out. The rungs were as old as the building itself: rusted, U-shaped, each one fastened with four nails directly onto the siding. The column of rungs reached all the way to the peak.

Tucker grabbed the lowest rung and tugged on it. A little loose. He stepped on it with one foot and bounced up and down. It wiggled, but felt like it would hold. He climbed a few more steps. The ninth rung was loose—two of the nails had rusted away—but the rungs were close enough together that he was able to climb past it. He looked down. A shame to waste all that climbing. He looked up. It wasn't that far. Kosh would never know.

He continued climbing. The top rung was about two feet below the eave, which jutted out from the siding. Two iron rails curved down around the overhang from the top, providing handholds. Grabbing one of the rails, Tucker gave it a hard yank. It felt secure. To get onto the roof, he would have to grab both rails and pull himself up. Tucker looked down.

*Whoa.* He squeezed his eyes closed and willed all of his strength into his hands. It was a *long* way down—he hadn't been this high since he'd tied the rope swing to the cottonwood. He waited for his heart to slow down, then moved his other hand to the rail, lifted one foot to the top rung, and pulled himself high enough to see the top of the roof.

The two rails, he was relieved to see, were fastened securely to the roof with shiny new bolts. Kosh must have been up there doing some maintenance. If it was safe for Kosh, who weighed well over two hundred pounds, it had to be safe for Tucker. Getting a new grip on the rails, Tucker pulled himself up onto the roof. He crawled on his belly along the ridge for a few feet to get away from the edge, then stood up.

About halfway along the ridge, between him and the weather vane, a shimmering, perfectly round distortion hovered four feet above the ridge. At close range, it looked like a pane of foggy, pulsing glass. Tucker edged forward, keeping one foot on either side of the ridge. He stopped ten feet short of the disk, wishing he had brought a stick or something to poke at it. He dug in his pockets and came out with his pocketknife. He moved closer, then tossed the knife at the disk.

The disk flashed orange; the knife disappeared.

Tucker got down on his hands and knees and looked at the roof on the other side of the disk. No knife. He crawled forward until his head was directly beneath the disk and looked up. Edge on, it became invisible, as if it had no third dimension. Keeping his head down, he crawled past the disk and stood up, gripping the weather vane for support. It looked exactly the same on the other side.

He was standing only three feet from the surface of the disk, close enough to feel it tugging at him, just like the one in Hopewell. His heart rate jumped from nervous and excited to flat-out scared. A voice inside his head was yelling at him to get away from the disk and off the roof, but before he could will his body to act, a prickling at the back of his ears made him turn to look behind him.

Three ghosts were floating around the weather vane, two men and a woman, all staring at him with colorless, translucent eyes. Tucker gasped and backed away from them. As he neared the surface of the disk, something grabbed him and squeezed— for an instant, he felt as if he'd been compressed to the size of a pea—then, with a sound like the final slurp of a milk shake through a straw, he was falling.

# 17  THE TOWERS

TUCKER LANDED HARD, FLAT ON HIS BACK. AIR EXPLODED from his lungs—for a moment, he thought he was back at Hardy Lake, slamming into the tree. He tried to breathe, but his chest was frozen and a sharp pain stabbed at his ears. Bubbles of black crowded the edges of his vision. Just as he felt himself slipping away, his chest suddenly expanded. Air flooded his lungs and his ears popped—the relief was exquisite, but short-lived, as the need for oxygen was replaced by a sharp pain in the small of his back.

*I fell off the barn,* he thought. *I've broken my back.*

He moved his right leg, then his left. Except for the knot of pain in his lower back he seemed to be okay. How far had he fallen? Forty, fifty feet? Turning his head, looking for the barn, he found only clear blue sky. He sat up. He was sitting on a flat, pebbly metal surface, painted blue-gray, bordered by a metal railing. Beyond the railing was the horizon: faint and distant, a blur of water touching the sky.

This was not Kosh's farm.

Tucker looked straight up. The wavering, not-quite-real shape of the disk hung eight feet above him, just out of reach. He climbed to his feet and noticed his folded pocketknife on the metal surface. That was what had been poking him in the back. He must have landed right on it.

He was on top of a building. He walked a few steps to the railing and looked out upon thousands of other buildings, most of them less than half as tall as the one he was standing upon. They looked like something Godzilla could crush with his great lizard feet. He looked down. His stomach lurched. Tiny cars crowded the city streets. Little dark specks — people — moved, antlike, along the sidewalks.

Turning to his left, he saw another incredibly tall building, maybe a hundred yards away, topped by the white spike of a giant antenna. The antenna alone was taller than any building in Hopewell.

To his right, beyond the sea of buildings, was a large body of water, its gray surface slashed by the white wakes of dozens of boats. He noticed an island with an oddly shaped, pointed structure jutting up from one end.

Every few yards along the railing, binocular telescopes were mounted on steel posts. Tucker tried to look through one, but saw nothing. He noticed a coin slot in the front of the telescope. He felt in his pockets, found two quarters, fed them in, heard a reassuring click, put his eyes to the scope, and aimed it at the island.

The pointy structure was a green metal statue. He had seen it before in pictures, and in movies.

The Statue of Liberty.

But the Statue of Liberty was in New York City.

How could he be in New York? He followed the railing. The city — uncountable buildings — spread out to the horizon. He noticed one building topped by a tall, graceful spire, not as tall as the building he was standing on, but taller than the rest. The Empire State Building? But there weren't any buildings taller than the Empire State Building in New York City, so how could he be looking *down* at it? He moved back from the railing and sat down on a green metal bench on the other side of the platform. He closed his eyes and hugged himself. This had to be a dream. When he opened his eyes the nightmare would be over. He would be back on Kosh's barn — unless that was part of the dream, too.

It all felt so real.

One, two, three . . . He would count to ten.

At the count of seven, Tucker became aware of a distant roar, growing rapidly louder. He opened his eyes and ran to the railing. An airplane, coming in low and astonishingly fast, was heading directly for the other building. Tucker watched it disappear behind the building. For one splinter of an instant he thought the plane had missed, then came a ripping, thudding explosion. A ball of flame blew out the side of the building. Less than a second later the shock wave hit, knocking Tucker back from the railing. The flames were followed by tremendous bloated cauli-flowers of black smoke writhing and twisting skyward.

Tucker jumped up and ran, following the railing around the edge of the platform, getting as far away from the burning building as he could. The choking black cloud quickly overtook him. He stopped running, pulled the neck of his T-shirt up over his mouth, and forced himself to think. He was sure about where he was now, even though it was impossible. The World Trade Center. Nine eleven. Tucker was too young to remember that day, but he had seen the videos.

He had to get off. There had to be an elevator or a stair-case someplace. Maybe he had time to get down before the second plane hit. He plunged forward, slitting his eyes against the stinging smoke. A clearing in the haze appeared; Tucker used the momentary respite to take several deep breaths. The plat-form turned to the left. He spotted an exit sign with an arrow pointing straight ahead. Another wave of dense smoke rolled over him, but he kept running, blinded — until he collided with something.

Something big. Tucker bounced off and fell back, hearing a gruff, startled exclamation.

Through the smoke, Tucker could see a large figure dressed in black standing over him. Tucker jumped up, relieved to find he was not alone.

"We have to get down!" he shouted.

"Tell me something I don't know, kid," the man said.

Tucker knew that voice.

"Kosh?"

The smoke thinned. Kosh Feye stood before him, his bright-blue eyes glowing in the smoke-muted sunlight.

"You know me?" Kosh grabbed the front of Tucker's T-shirt. "Who are you?"

"You *know* who I am!"

Kosh stared hard at him for three heartbeats. He looked different. Younger. His nose wasn't all pushed to the side, and his eyebrows were solid, thick, and jet black.

"I've seen you someplace," Kosh said.

"Yeah, like this morning."

Kosh let go of Tucker's shirt and shook his head. "Yeah, right. Whatever. Listen, kid—whoever you are—the elevators are shut down, and the doors to the escalators are locked. I've been trying to get out of this nightmare for ten minutes." Another cloud of oily smoke rolled over them. Tucker crouched, getting down low so he could breathe. Kosh stared at him, unaffected by the smoke. "How'd you get here?"

"I don't know. I was on your roof—"

"*My* roof? What were you—?"

"And I saw this, like, fuzzy place in the air, and it slurped me up."

"Slurped?"

"That's what it felt like."

"I thought it felt more like being shot out of a cannon."

"You went through too?"

"I was putting up my new weather vane. And *pow,* I end up here. You know where we are, don't you?"

"The World Trade Center?"

"Right. September eleven. But that's impossible. The towers fell last week."

"Last week? It was *years* ago."

"Years? You got a pretty weak grasp of recent history, kid. It happened last Tuesday."

"If it happened last Tuesday, then how can we be standing here now?"

"You got me. All I know is, if we don't wake up from this nightmare soon, we aren't going to wake up at all. There were two of them, you know. Two planes. The second plane hit about twenty minutes after the first one. How long you figure it's been? Ten, fifteen minutes?"

"Maybe we're here for a reason," Tucker said. "Maybe we can do something. Warn everybody to get out?"

"Kid, there isn't a single person in either of these buildings who isn't already trying to get out."

"But—we can't just have come here to *die.*"

"Maybe we're *already* dead."

"Not yet," Tucker said, thinking about the disk. Maybe it was still there. Maybe it worked both ways. "I might know a way off."

"What, jump? No thanks."

"We can go back the way we came," Tucker said. "That thing that brought us here, if we can find it, maybe it'll take us back."

"Thing? I didn't see any *thing*."

"It's like a disk. I saw it. Come on!" They followed the railing around the observation deck. The wind had shifted, blowing the smoke across the far side of the building. Tucker was walking with his head tipped back, looking for the disk. He stopped.

"There."

"Where?"

Tucker pointed up.

"I don't see anything," Kosh said.

It was faint, but Tucker could see it: a disk-shaped slice of thicker, denser, fuzzier air.

Tucker grabbed Kosh's sleeve and pulled him to a spot directly beneath it. "Reach straight up, as high as you can."

Kosh raised his arm. The tips of his fingers came to within a few inches of the bottom of the circle.

"You're almost touching it," Tucker said.

"I feel —" Kosh jerked his hand back. "Something grabbed at my fingers!"

"Can you see it? You have to focus on it just right."

Kosh backed up a few steps, squinting. "Like a big fuzzy circle?"

"That's it."

"And you think that's how we got here?"

"All we got to do is get up there and go through. I think."

Kosh was gazing off to the west, across the Hudson River, where a silver speck glittered just above the horizon.

"Flight 175, right on schedule," he said.

"Your stepladder!" Tucker said.

"Stepladder?" Kosh's eyes were fixed on the approaching jetliner.

"You got a stepladder in the barn, right?"

"So?"

"Lift me up. I'll send you back a ladder so you can get up there."

"You're talking to a dead man," said Kosh. "Say your prayers, kid. Once that plane hits, it won't be long before this thing goes down."

"How long?"

Kosh shook his head. "I don't know. Maybe half an hour?"

Tucker grabbed Kosh's arm. "Then we don't have much time. Boost me up!"

Kosh looked down at him.

"Come *on*!"

Kosh lifted Tucker onto his shoulders.

"Higher," said Tucker. He got one foot on Kosh's right shoulder as Kosh pushed up on his buttocks. He stood, shakily, one foot on each of Kosh's broad shoulders, looking directly into the circle of mist.

"Here it comes," said Kosh. "Hang on, kid."

"Look for the ladder," Tucker said.

There was an ear-crushing roar, the building shuddered and swayed, and Tucker dove headfirst into the disk.

**18   LADDERS**

Tucker hit the barn roof and felt himself start to slide. His right hand closed around something—one of the support brackets for the weather vane. He hung on, waiting a few seconds for his heart to slow. His eardrums felt as if they had been pierced by needles. Tucker swallowed, and his ears popped as the pressure equalized. He pulled himself back onto the ridge. The surface of the disk wavered and swam hungrily. The ghosts he had seen before were gone. He ducked under the disk and ran along the ridge. Seconds later, he was scrambling down the rungs.

After being on top of the World Trade Center, forty feet up the side of a barn was nothing. He hit the ground running. Kosh's extension ladder was leaning against the south wall. That wouldn't work—he needed the stepladder, which could stand by itself, so Kosh could use it to reach the disk. He ran inside and climbed the spiral staircase to the top floor, and found the six-foot aluminum stepladder next to a pile of studs.

The ladder wasn't heavy, but it was awkward. He felt as if he was moving in slow motion as he dragged it down the spiral staircase. Once outside, he started up the iron rungs with the stepladder digging painfully into his shoulder. Halfway up, his leg cramped. He rested the bottom of the ladder on a rung and held it there with one hand while he shook out his leg, willing the calf muscle to relax.

*Plenty of time,* he told himself, not knowing if it was true. He continued up the side of the barn, the ladder clanking over the iron rungs.

Once he reached the top, he had to get the stepladder over his shoulder and onto the roof. It had seemed so light when he first picked it up; now it weighed a ton. He tried to lift it over his head one-handed but couldn't. He needed three hands — one to hang on to the ladder, and two to pull himself onto the roof.

Tucker spewed out a string of expletives he had recently learned from Kosh. It didn't help. He took his right foot off the rung and tried to swing the ladder between himself and the barn, his idea being to somehow hang it from one of the rungs, but the ladder slipped from his grip, hit his left ankle, and left him dangling by one hand as it crashed to the ground.

Grabbing the railing with his other hand, Tucker found the rungs with his feet. His heart was banging so hard, he could feel it in his throat. He tried to move, to unclench his hands from the rails. It took some time — seconds that felt like hours — but eventually he was able to climb back down.

The aluminum ladder was bent, but not too badly. It was still usable. He ran to Kosh's workshop and located a coil of nylon rope. He tied one end to the ladder and the other to his belt, then again scaled the side of the barn — just like dragging the heavy rope up the cottonwood at Hardy Lake. When he reached the top, he pulled the stepladder up hand-over-hand, then dragged it over the edge and onto the roof. But the disk was gone.

How could it be *gone*? He ran along the ridge to where the disk had been. Had it moved? He looked around frantically but saw nothing.

"No!" he shouted.

As if someone had heard his cry, the air before him wavered and thickened. Tucker jumped back. He could feel it tugging at his shirt front. He backed along the ridge to where he had left the ladder. The disk shimmered and pulsed. He dragged the ladder over, set it upright, and tipped the top end toward the disk. The instant it touched the surface, there was a brilliant orange flash and the ladder was ripped from Tucker's hands. He shouted with pain and surprise. It had been snatched away with such speed and force that strips of skin were torn from his palms.

Pressing his injured hands together, Tucker stared fiercely into the disk. All he could do now was hope. If the ladder had reached Kosh in time, he should come popping out of the disk any second. But if the towers had already collapsed, the ladder would materialize in midair and fall onto a pile of burning, smoking wreckage.

He backed away, making room for Kosh's arrival.

He waited.

After a few minutes, he sat down, trying not to think about the pain in his hands.

If only Kosh would hurry.

Tucker thought about all those people, the unseen thousands within the tower. He had been a toddler back then. He had no real memories of the disaster. It had always seemed like a piece of history to him, as distant as World War II or Elvis Presley. When he had watched videos of the attack it hadn't felt much different from watching movies where things get blown up every ten minutes. Not real. But now it was a part of him forever. Because he had been there.

He had never felt so alone, not even when his parents had left him.


Tucker stayed on the roof until the sun was low in the sky and all hope had drained away. He had been too late, too slow. The towers had collapsed. Kosh was dead.

As he climbed down the side of the barn, gripping the iron rungs gingerly with his torn palms, a vast, poisonous emptiness filled his gut. Each rung seemed to make Kosh's death more certain, more real. He had failed. If only he had not dropped the ladder. If he had been stronger. Faster.

Tucker was squatting at the hose spigot, running cool water over his injured hands, when he heard the rumble of an approaching motorcycle. He looked up and saw a Harley coming up the driveway. Kosh!

He forgot about his injured hands and ran to meet him. Kosh pulled up, put down his kickstand, dismounted, and took off his helmet. Tucker threw his arms around his uncle, then immediately realized what he was doing, let go, and backed off a few steps. Kosh stood gaping at him.

"You okay, kid? You look like you've seen a ghost."

Tucker's mouth was moving, but no sound came out.

Kosh leaned in close and sniffed. "What did you burn down this time?"

"Where . . . ?" Tucker shook his head, staring at Kosh, trying to make sense of the impossible. Kosh's eyebrows were missing again, and his nose had returned to its flattened, off-center appearance. "Where'd you come from?"

"I told you. I was up in Eau Claire," Kosh said. "You sure you're—wait a sec." He leaned in to take another sniff, stepped back, and looked up at the barn roof. "You've been up there, haven't you?"

Tucker nodded.

"I knew it." He grabbed Tucker by the shoulders and locked eyes with him. "Tell me where you were," he said in a tight voice.

"I was . . . I was with you."

*"Where?"*

"At the — on the — up on the top of the tower —"

Kosh released him and threw up his arms and looked skyward. "Praise God, I'm not crazy after all. It really happened!" He looked at Tucker. "World Trade Center, right?"

Tucker nodded.

"Nine eleven?"

"Yeah."

"Man! I thought it was a dream!" Kosh was walking in tight circles, waving his arms and talking fast. "But it was so real, everything! The smoke . . . I was coughing for days. The doctors told me it was the fall. The *fall*? Falling off a barn doesn't make you smell like burning jet fuel, now, does it? I can't believe this."

He slapped Tucker on the back, sending him staggering. Tucker fell onto his hands and let fly a howl of pain.

"What did you do to your hands? Let me have a look. Ouch! C'mon inside. Let's get you bandaged up, okay?"

Kosh didn't stop talking the whole time he was cleaning and bandaging Tucker's palms. "Thought it was bees at first," he said. "I was just finishing putting up the weather vane and heard this buzzing behind me. I turned around and looked, but I didn't see anything except maybe a little waviness in the air, like heat rising off a hot highway, you know? Then I felt this weird reverse wind, like instead of blowing against me it was sucking at me. And then — *bam* — I'm on the tower. Thought I was having a psychotic episode. Then I ran into you — 'course, I didn't know you at the time — and I was sure of it. The psychotic episode, I mean."

"I sent you a ladder."

"You sure did! I remember you were on my shoulders, and then the second plane hit, and you were gone, and the smoke—so much smoke—and the heat coming up over the edge, and I'm thinking it's the end." He paused. "Then I hear this clatter and I see this stepladder lying on the deck, like it'd been there all along."

"Your ladder. That's how I tore up my hands."

Kosh finished wrapping Tucker's right hand. "How does that feel?"

"Better."

"Good." Kosh sat back. "The weird thing is, back in 2001, my stepladder was this rickety old wooden job. I just bought the aluminum one last year. Anyway, I set that ladder up and climbed up it and next thing I knew I was rolling down the barn roof." He put a finger to his nose. "That's how I got this nose. Broke my collarbone and a couple ribs, too. Then I made the mistake of telling the docs what happened. Psychotic break brought on by post-traumatic stress, they said. I spent a month in the psych ward, trying to convince them I wasn't some kind of dangerous lunatic."

"A month? But I just—"

"This was in 2001, don't forget. I came back the same time I left."

"I don't get it."

"Me neither." Kosh closed his eyes, then opened them. "But I've been thinking about it ever since. I mean, if it was real—and I'm not so sure it was—I might have had time to save some of those people. I might have used the ladder to break through the doors and get some of them out. But all I could think of was getting off that roof."

"Anybody would be scared."

"Didn't say I was scared."

"Well, *I* was. Anyway, you didn't have time to save anybody."

"Maybe not."

"I'm just glad we got off."

Kosh put his hands on Tucker's shoulders and looked into his eyes. "Look, I don't know what happened, but I'm pretty sure I wouldn't be alive if it wasn't for you. I owe you one. I got a bad feeling about that . . . whatever it is."

"Maybe it's a time portal. Or a wormhole," Tucker said, lifting the terms from a movie he had seen.

"Call it what you want. I want nothing to do with it."

"I mean, we both went through, and the ladder went through, and we both ended up at the same time and place. But when we went through it backward, it took us to where we each started from." Tucker took a breath. A thought had been slowly solidifying in his brain. Maybe the thing he'd seen on the roof back in Hopewell was another time portal. Maybe that was what happened to his dad the day he had disappeared. . . .

**19 IT NEVER HAPPENED**

"How are you going to get up there if you have to fix the roof or something?" Tucker asked.

"Let it leak," Kosh said.

Tucker backed away from the barn to where he could see the peak. The satellite dish was there, but the disk, wormhole— whatever—was not visible.

"It's not there," he said.

"It's been gone before. I'm taking no chances," Kosh said. He looked up at his handiwork. The bottom fifteen rungs were gone. "Guess I don't have to take them all off." He climbed down and collected the rungs, hanging them over his forearm as he picked them up.

Tucker said, "Shouldn't we tell somebody about it?"

"Tell who?"

"NASA? The FBI? The Highway Department?"

"The Highway Department?"

"Well . . . it's transportation, right?"

Kosh shook his head. "Believe me, we do not want to get the government involved in this."

"But maybe they could figure out a way to save the towers. Go back in time with an antiaircraft gun and shoot the planes down."

"Not gonna happen."

"Why not?"

Kosh ticked off points on his thick fingers: "First, it's a done deal. The towers collapsed, and that's that. You go back and change that—even if you *could* change it, which I don't think you can—then everything from then on would be different. You'd be a completely different person. And second, if you were a different person, then none of this would've happened in the first place." He raised his nonexistent eyebrows, daring Tucker to prove him wrong.

"So we just do nothing?"

"What we do is, we stay off that roof." Kosh looked at the rungs hanging on his arm. He walked over to the rusting pile of scrap metal by the corner of the barn and dumped them on top of a bunch of empty beer cans. "As far as I'm concerned, it never happened."

"What never happened?"

Kosh jerked his thumb toward the roof.

Tucker was confused. "What do you mean?"

"I mean we forget about it. Get on with our lives."

"But—"

"No *buts*. I don't want to spend the rest of my life in a

mental institution or chained to a wall in a CIA dungeon, and I *especially* do not want to spend the rest of my life dead."

"But—"

"But nothing. I been in a straitjacket once, and that's one time too many. Case closed." He crossed his arms and regarded Tucker. "How are your hands?"

"They're okay."

"Good. Anybody asks you what happened, say you fell off your bike."

The next day, over a breakfast of pancakes and bacon, Tucker tried again to talk to Kosh about the tower, but Kosh said, "That's ancient history, kid."

"Ancient history? It was yesterday!"

"I don't want to talk about it," Kosh said.

"You're worse than my dad," Tucker said. "He used to say that all the time."

"Maybe he had his reasons."

Frustrated, Tucker finished his breakfast and went outside. He looked up at the roof. No disk. Maybe it was gone for good. And maybe Kosh could pretend it had never happened, but Tucker knew better—the disk had been real. Furthermore, he was sure there had been another one in Hopewell, on the roof of his house. The one that had caused his father to disappear. But disappear to where? Not the World Trade Center. And he had not returned through the disk but had come walking up the road with Lahlia. That might mean there was yet *another* disk—and that Lahlia had come from some place that was certainly not Bulgaria. Some place with pyramids and priests and a "blood moon," she had said that day at the swing.

He thought about the misty people he had seen floating above the barn, and in Hopewell. Ghosts? Angels? They had not looked very angelic. No wings, or halos, or radiating goodness. His mom believed in angels, but she said she had been seeing "ghosts."

He didn't know *what* they were. Lahlia had called them Klaatu. Tucker was becoming convinced that the disks, Lahlia, and the ghosts were all connected. And maybe his parents' disappearance, too.

He had to return to Hopewell.

Back inside, Tucker followed sounds of hammering to the third floor, where he found Kosh balanced precariously on a sawhorse, installing a strip of bead board in the ceiling.

"How's it going?" Tucker asked.

Kosh turned his head to look at Tucker, lost his balance, and slipped. His hammer fell to the floor, and he landed with one foot on either side of the sawhorse and let out a string of curses.

"Good thing that sawhorse isn't six inches taller," said Tucker.

Kosh looked down at the two inches of space between his crotch and the bar of the sawhorse and cursed some more.

"And I can't find my damn stepladder," he said. Tucker

opened his mouth to explain, thinking that the missing ladder would surely prove to Kosh that they had really been to the World Trade Center, but what he saw in his uncle's face stopped him cold.

Tucker's big, fearsome, seemingly invulnerable uncle was afraid.

"I guess I got to drive into town and buy a new one," Kosh said.

"There's a ladder in the garage at home," Tucker said. "Why don't we go get it?"

"Drive two hours for a ladder? No way."

"We could check on the house, make sure everything's okay."

Kosh was not convinced.

Tucker said, "Tell you what: I'll drive."

"You? You won't be street legal for another two years. If we go—and I'm not saying we're *going*, because we *aren't*—I'm driving. You clear?"

"Okay," Tucker said.

Kosh picked up his hammer and climbed back onto the sawhorse.

"My dad has an electric nail gun," Tucker said. "I bet it would make that job go a lot faster."

"I don't need a nail gun," said Kosh, and promptly smashed his thumb with the hammer.

**20 HOPEWELL, AGAIN**

Except for the tall grass and half a dozen soggy copies of the *Hopewell Shopper* on the front steps, the house was much as they had left it. Kosh immediately raided the garage for tools. Tucker examined the roof. He walked around the house to view it from different angles. He saw no sign of the disk. After a few minutes, he went through the house to search for any signs that his parents had been there. He found a dead mouse in the toilet, spiderwebs in every corner, and thousands of box-elder bugs. Other than that, everything was as he had left it.

He gathered some odds and ends — books, a handheld video game that needed a battery, a few articles of clothing — loaded them into a cardboard box, and carried them outside.

Kosh was standing beside the car, talking to a girl with blond hair. The girl turned toward Tucker.

"Hello, Tucker Feye," said Lahlia.

Her hair was longer and was coming in darker yellow, more the color of corn than of corn silk. The summer sun had tinted her face a pale bronze, making her eyelashes look almost white. She was dressed in loose jeans and a black T-shirt with a pink skull and crossbones printed on the front. Above the skull were the words *Eat Vegan or Die.* He noticed that she filled out her T-shirt more than he remembered, and she seemed taller.

"Nice shirt," he said, staring at her chest.

"Arnold and Maria find it disturbing."

"I guess that makes sense, them being dairy farmers and all."

"They are ignorant, but not unkind. Primitive people believe that by eating animal flesh they can take on the qualities of the creature they are consuming. Fortunately, Maria no longer tries to put dead animal parts into my food."

"Animal parts?" That sounded disgusting. He imagined Maria Becker hiding a chicken gizzard inside a brownie. "Like what?"

"She would add broth made from dead roosters to my soup, and fried chips of smoked hog flesh to my salad."

Kosh, who had been listening with an amused smile, laughed. "Chicken stock and bacon never sounded so bad," he said. He headed back to the garage for more tools. A small gray cat appeared from beneath the lilac bushes, trotted over to Lahlia, and rubbed its cheek on her ankle. She bent over and picked it up.

"That isn't the same cat you had before, is it?" Tucker said.

"Yes. This is Bounce."

"Shouldn't he be bigger? He still looks like a kitten."

Lahlia stroked Bounce's fine gray fur. "Maria says he's a runt. Arnold and Maria have larger cats. Bounce doesn't like them. He follows me everywhere."

"Where did he come from, anyways?"

"He came with you."

"What? I think I'd know if we'd had a cat in the car."

"I don't mean today. Later, he will come with you."

Tucker shook his head, confused. Kosh returned from the garage, carrying another armload of tools.

"You'll see," Lahlia said. She turned to Kosh. "Have you returned to Hopewell to stay?"

"Just a visit," said Kosh. He held up Adrian Feye's nail gun. "We're picking up a few things." He looked at Tucker. "Lahlia tells me the new preacher is even crazier than Adrian," he said to Tucker.

"My dad's not crazy," he said.

Kosh shrugged. "Maybe so, but this new guy . . . Tell him, Lahlia."

"Father September preaches that computers are the source of all evil. He performs miracles. He made Mrs. Friedman walk again."

"See what I mean?" said Kosh with a smirk.

"Arnold doesn't like him. Arnold says if God puts you in a wheelchair, you should darn well stay there."

"That's crazy," Tucker said.

"Arnold eats many chickens," Lahlia replied. "I once drank mammal milk. Maria insisted. It was quite odd."

"You should try it with chocolate in it," Tucker said.

Lahlia smiled. "I like chocolate."

Kosh, fitting the tools into the trunk of the car, said, "Everybody likes chocolate." Head still in the trunk, he said, "You got everything you need, Tucker?"

"I guess so." Tucker looked again at the roof, wondering how he could convince Kosh to hang around for a while longer.

As they were fitting the last few items into the car, a beat-up Toyota pickup truck drove by, skidded to a halt, backed up, and turned into the driveway. The pickup pulled up behind the Chevy, and Ronnie Becker got out. He looked the same as he had the day Tucker had seen him at Hardy Lake: long black hair, black jeans, and a studded leather vest. He walked up to Kosh, grinning.

"Kosh Feye. Long time, bro." He held up his fist. Kosh gave him a halfhearted fist bump. "Haven't seen you since you left me in — where was it? Flagstaff? How you been?"

"I'm good," said Kosh.

They stood a few feet apart, looking at each other.

Ronnie said, "What happened to your eyebrows?"

"Lost 'em," Kosh said.

"Looks like you busted your nose, too."

Kosh shrugged. "What are you doing back in town, Ronnie?"

Tucker got the impression that Kosh and Ronnie had not parted on the best of terms.

"Helping the old folks out," Ronnie said. "Arnold's just as cranky as ever. You?"

"Just picking up some stuff. We were getting ready to leave."

"Yeah, I don't know how much longer I'll last here in Hopeless myself," Ronnie said. He turned to Lahlia. "Maria's been looking for you."

Bounce flattened his ears and hissed.

Ronnie grimaced. "That cat never liked me."

"Bounce is an excellent judge of character," Lahlia said.

"Yeah, well, Maria's on the warpath. She'll make you sit through a doubleheader at church come Sunday if you don't get on top of that berry patch. You don't pick them now they'll be bird food tomorrow."

"Birds have to eat too," Lahlia said.

"Whatever you say." He turned to Kosh. "Want to run into town? Grab a beer at the Drop? We're old enough now — Red will probably serve us."

Kosh hesitated.

"It's been a long time, bro," Ronnie said. "We got a lot of catching up to do."

Kosh looked at Tucker.

"I'll be okay on my own," Tucker said quickly. "Lahlia and I have some catching up to do, too."

"What do we have to catch up to?" Lahlia asked.

Ronnie laughed. "Little Miss Literal."

"Seriously, go ahead," Tucker said to Kosh. "I'll finish packing some things."

Kosh pressed his lips together, then nodded slowly. "There's a cooler in the car with some sandwiches if you get hungry."

"Okay."

"We won't be long." Ronnie crossed his heart and grinned. The two men walked over to Ronnie's pickup truck and got in. Seconds later, Tucker was alone with Lahlia. She was staring at him with her enormous dark eyes. Bounce launched himself from her arms and bounded off after a grasshopper.

"Your uncle Kosh is a fearful man," Lahlia said.

"You think he's scary?"

"I think he's afraid. Why else would he wear armor?"

"Armor?"

"His animal skins," she said.

"You mean his leathers? That's just so people will think he's this big tough biker."

"He's afraid of people thinking he's afraid."

"You talk different now," Tucker said.

"I'm using what you call contractions. Ronnie told me I talked like a robot. He is not very nice. Kosh is nice. He worries about you."

"He's okay," Tucker said. A feeling of sadness swept across him; his eyes stung. "He reminds me of my dad sometimes." He looked away. "I miss my parents."

The intensity of Lahlia's gaze increased. "You don't know where they are?"

"They went . . . away. That's why I've been staying with Kosh."

"Did they go away because your mother was ill?"

"I think so." Tucker felt something change, like a silent electrical discharge, or a sudden variation in the barometric pressure. They both turned to look up at the roof.

The disk was back, hovering just off the peak.

"The Gate does not come often," Lahlia said. "It does not stay long."

"You came out of it, didn't you?" Tucker said. "You and my dad."

"No. There is another."

"Another one? Where?"

She pointed toward downtown Hopewell. "Your father found me there."

"So he *did* go through one of those things?"

"Yes."

"Do you know where he is?"

Lahlia stared at his face, her eyes making small jumps from his eyes to his mouth to his nose, as if trying to fix his every feature in her mind. She pointed up at the shimmering disk.

**21  PASSAGES**

TUCKER FELT HIMSELF MAKING A DECISION — A LOOSEN-ing in his gut and a lightness in his head — the same feeling he had had the first time he went off the rope swing.

The disk might disappear again at any moment. He ran to the garage, lifted the aluminum extension ladder from its hangers, and carried it to the house. If he thought too much about what he was about to do, he might freeze up. He leaned the ladder against the eave, and climbed. Seconds later, he was standing on the roof looking into the disk. The surface buzzed and hummed; swirling gray clouds pressed against a perfectly flat, transparent membrane. He hesitated, fear and common sense battling with his need to act.

"You will not be welcome," Lahlia said. She was on the roof, standing a few paces behind him, holding Bounce in her arms. "They may attempt to kill you."

"Who will?" Tucker asked.

"The priests. You will know them by their yellow robes."

Tucker looked from Lahlia to the disk.

"Priests in yellow robes? So there's a church or something on the other side?"

"There is an altar atop the pyramid at the center of Romelas, the great city of the Lah Sept."

Her words made no sense. Tucker understood only one thing. "But my parents are there?"

"Only your father." Bounce's yellow eyes were fixed upon the disk, his tail twitching.

"How do you know that?"

"I was there."

The disk changed subtly, going from swirling clouds to grainy salt and pepper with a faint green tinge. The surface bulged; several gaseous shapes emerged, skinless balloons of white mist. Tucker stepped back, his heart hammering in his ears, as the shapes metamorphosed into transparent human figures hovering at various heights on either side of the disk.

"Do you see them?" he asked.

*"Klaatu!"* said Lahlia. Her eyes were huge. Bounce was making a peculiar sound somewhere between a mewl and a yowl.

The mist peoples' features moved in and out of focus as more of them emerged from the disk, men and women, all looking expectantly at Tucker. One of them, a man with round features and small eyes, drifted closer. Tucker batted at it with his hand. He felt nothing, but the gaseous shape fragmented where his hand passed through. The broken mist man drifted away, then re-formed.

"What do they *want*?" Tucker's voice cracked.

"They come at moments of terror and triumph," Lahlia said. Bounce hissed at the ghostly shapes, digging his claws into her arms. "They are hungry for drama."

There were more than a dozen of the mist people hovering on either side of Tucker and Lahlia, staying just out of reach. Tucker tried to focus on their individual faces, but when he looked at any one of them straight on, their features softened and blurred. The surface of the disk had changed from grainy green to a cloudy, colorless whirlpool. Bounce squirmed and growled, then let out a horrific screech and exploded from Lahlia's arms. He hit the roof and made a panicked dash for the edge — straight at the disk.

"Bounce! *No!*" Lahlia shouted.

Tucker tried to grab the cat, but it shot between his legs. Off balance, Tucker stumbled and fell forward. The cat leaped. The disk flashed orange. Bounce disappeared into the whorl.

Tucker, on his hands and knees, was facing the disk from inches away. He felt it sucking at him, a thousand invisible fingers tugging at his clothing, at his skin, at every hair on his body. He gripped the rough shingles with his hands and tried to push himself back, but the wind had him in its grip. He could hear Lahlia shouting something, but her words were garbled. Slowly, inch by inch, the disk drew him closer until, with the same gulping, slurping sound he remembered from before, he was swallowed up.

\* \* \*

Lahlia stood on the roof and watched the Klaatu drift toward the Gate, their ethereal forms distorting and streaming into the disk like wisps of smoke entering an exhaust fan. The Gate buzzed and flickered. She heard the faint hiss and rattle of wind passing through leaves, and the distant lowing of slave cattle. Turning slowly, she looked out over the land surrounding Tucker Feye's childhood home. A place of legend. She looked toward downtown Hopewell. A figure in black was walking up the road.

Kosh.

She watched him grow slowly larger. Soon, she could make out the details of his face—the missing eyebrows, the off-center nose, the set of his mouth.

Standing before the Gate, she waited for him.

It was strange spending time with Ronnie Becker. Kosh had thought about him often since they'd split up after a month of vagabonding around the West on their motorcycles. They'd had a lot of fun until that one night when they got in a drunken argument that ended with a bloody nose for Ronnie. Kosh had ridden off on his bike, leaving Ronnie sitting on a curb outside a bar in Flagstaff.

They'd been little more than kids—immature, impulsive, and stupid. That was a long time ago. They were older now. They were men. They could laugh about it. He told Ronnie about falling off the barn, breaking his nose and collarbone, somehow making it funny, but leaving out the part about the disk and the World Trade Center. Ronnie told Kosh about some of his adventures: a brief period of living with a group of Hare Krishnas in Denver, a month in the county jail in Albuquerque — Ronnie wouldn't say what that was for — and two years as a deacon in an evangelical mega-church in Nebraska. He'd been kicked out of the church after getting caught in a motel room with the preacher's teenage daughter. Ronnie had always had a knack for trouble. Now he was back, living with his parents, but he said it wouldn't be for long. He'd gotten a job working for the new preacher.

"The miracle cure dude?" Kosh asked.

"You got it, bro." Ronnie winked. "My ticket to heaven."

After one beer, Kosh said he should be getting back to Tucker. Ronnie wanted to keep drinking and talking.

"One beer? Since when does Kosh Feye stop at one?"

Kosh stood up. "Sorry, man, I gotta go."

He left Ronnie at the bar with Henry Hall, who would drink and talk with anybody, and walked back to his brother's house. It was a relief to leave Ronnie behind — again.

As he walked up the driveway toward the house, Kosh noticed Lahlia on the roof. And a few feet in front of her, floating just off the peak, was the faint outline of a disk.

The fear rose up inside him. "Don't get too close to that thing!" he shouted.

Lahlia gave him a small wave, stepped off the edge of the roof, and was gone.

Kosh stood frozen, staring up at the empty space where the

girl had been, hearing his own breathing and the pounding of his heart. Then something inside him broke free, and he was climbing the ladder, running along the roof ridge toward the disk. He stopped himself just in time. The disk hummed and crackled with malevolent energy.

Taking a step back, Kosh tried to think. Whatever was happening, it was real. Either that or he was truly insane. What was he supposed to do? Follow the girl into the disk? He was certain that Tucker had preceded her. He should have known. He should never have left him. The kid had as much as told him that he thought Adrian and Emily had been swallowed by a disk. Kosh hadn't taken him seriously. It made no sense, but Tucker was a teenager with the same reckless disregard for his own safety as Kosh had at that age.

Could he follow them? Would it do any good? Or would it be like jumping into a volcano? He would take a bullet to save Tucker — to save any kid. But this thing — this disk — it terrified him to the depths of his soul.

With that realization there came a faint hissing sound; the fuzzy surface of the disk turned clear, then disappeared completely. Kosh reached out with his hand, but felt nothing.

He sat down on the ridge with his back against the chimney and waited there for a very long time. The disk did not reappear.

# PART THREE

# THE CYDONIAN PYRAMID

*In theory, it was not possible for a Klaatu to feel tired. With no physical body, there could be no accumulation of waste products in the bloodstream, no muscle fatigue, no drowsiness, no hunger, no thirst. To be a Klaatu was—in theory—to experience every moment in a state of blissful awareness.*

*Nevertheless, as the millennia passed, many of the Klaatu became inexplicably listless and torpid. Attempts by the Cluster to reenergize these "tired" Klaatu were not entirely successful. Those afflicted showed no desire to reignite their vitality. Efforts to engage them were greeted with apathy and the Klaatu version of sighs. Some feared that the tired would slowly fade until their consciousnesses dissipated completely.*

*A few Klaatu theorized that such dissipation would lead to another form of transcendence, but none of them was willing to put it to the test.*

*The artist and disko designer Iyl Rayn, who had never questioned her own vitality, one day discovered within herself the weariness of a traveler who has reached the midway point of an arduous journey, the purpose of which has been long forgotten. Fearing that she herself was becoming tired, she once again called upon the corporeal Boggsians for their technical expertise, directing them to employ the diskos to obtain a sample of her original corporeal DNA.*

— $E^3$

## 22   THE FRUSTUM

Tucker landed on his hands and knees on a hard stone surface. The stone was warm, like a sun-baked sidewalk, but this was no sidewalk — the surface was sandpaper rough, made of close-fitting limestone blocks.

He sat back on his knees. It was night. He was looking down a steep, stepped wall of stone blocks, wider at the bottom than at the top. To either side of him, burning torches were affixed to ten-foot-tall poles set into the top step. The disk from which he had fallen floated in the air just above him, so close that he could have reached out and touched it.

Far below, at the base of the stepped wall, thousands of people crowded an enormous plaza, torchlight reflecting off their upturned faces. He felt rather than heard their voices, a thrumming in the thick, humid air.

Other voices, close and angry, came from behind him. Tucker turned. He was on the edge of a stone platform about thirty feet across. Four more disks, just like the one he had fallen from, hovered over the other sides of the platform, each of them flanked by a pair of tall torches. At the center of the platform was a waist-high block of black stone. An altar? A pale-haired girl was standing upon it — Lahlia! But she looked younger, her hair was shorter, and she had on the same silvery shift she had worn the day she had arrived in Hopewell. Her feet were bare.

A flash of gray caught his eye. Bounce leaped from the platform onto the altar and into Lahlia's arms. The two of them stared down at Tucker — Lahlia in wide-eyed astonishment, as if she had never seen him before, while Bounce watched him with slitted, knowing yellow eyes, his tail twitching.

On the other side of the altar, near the far edge of the platform, three men in hooded yellow robes were crowded together, bent over something. They had their backs to him and had not seen him arrive. Were these the priests Lahlia had mentioned? Two of them had their hoods up; the third had his hood down, revealing a shaven scalp and a scraggly beard. They were speaking in a strange language.

Tucker couldn't see what it was they were looking at — the stone altar blocked his view. Lahlia, hugging her cat to her chest, looked terrified. Tucker edged to his left to see what had the priests' attention. A figure was sprawled limply at the edge of the platform, wearing jeans and a flannel shirt.

"Dad!" He cried out without thinking.

The priests looked up, startled.

Forgetting Lahlia's warnings about the priests, Tucker

dashed across the platform to his father. The Reverend Feye's eyes were half-closed and unfocused. Tucker shook him.

"Dad! Wake up!"

One of the priests grabbed Tucker by his collar. Tucker twisted free and backed away.

"What did you do to him?" he shouted.

The bearded priest, a dark-eyed man with harsh, hawklike features, answered him with a string of nonsense words that sounded like a mixture of Chinese and Spanish.

"Speak English!" Tucker said. "I can't understand you."

The priest raised his black eyebrows. *"¿Inglés?"* he said, pointing a short black baton at Tucker.

Tucker backed away. The bearded priest lunged toward him, jabbing the baton at him. Tucker dodged the thrust, looking around frantically. He kept backing away from the priest, following the edge of the platform. Each of the sides ended in a long, widening series of steps down to the crowded plaza—he realized that he was on top of an enormous, five-sided pyramid. Other than jumping into one of the disks, the only way off was to climb down the sides, but the pyramid was completely surrounded by the crowd of people.

The priests were coming at him from both sides. Tucker grasped one of the torch poles, pulled it free, and swung it at the nearest one. The priest jumped back, tripped, and fell over the edge, screaming as he tumbled down the steep side of the pyramid. Tucker swung the torch back toward the other two priests, but before he could swing again, the bearded priest rushed in and chopped at the torch with his baton. The baton struck with an explosion of blue sparks; the torch separated from the pole and fell smoking to the platform.

The priest gestured with the baton and said something, again in the strange language. The other priest had circled the platform and was coming up behind Tucker. Tucker swung the broken pole from side to side, trying to keep them both at bay.

While the priests were focused on Tucker, Lahlia had climbed down from the altar and moved toward the far side of the platform, carrying Bounce. She stopped in front of the disk nearest Tucker's unconscious father and looked back at Tucker and the two priests.

Bounce yowled.

The bearded priest looked back at her and shouted something. Lahlia shook her head and, with an expression that was both terrified and triumphant, stepped into the disk. The disk flashed orange, and she was gone.

The priest cried out in frustration, then turned back toward Tucker, his face contorted with anger. Tucker jabbed at him with the broken end of the torch pole. The priest knocked it aside contemptuously and touched the baton to Tucker's hand. A jolt of pure pain rocketed up Tucker's arm and exploded at the base of his skull. Every muscle in his body went slack, and he collapsed to the stone platform.

A hypnotic, almost subsonic murmur from the crowd below filled the air. Tucker could see and hear, but he could not move.

The priests standing over him were speaking more gibberish. The bearded one gestured at Tucker's father, a few yards away, and said something that sounded like *"Heid."* Tucker could see the two priests drag his father across the platform. Each priest took an arm and a leg, lifted him, and threw him into one of the disks. Another orange flash, and his father was gone.

The priests returned to Tucker, dragged him to the altar, and set him roughly upon it. Unable to move his head, Tucker stared up into a star-pocked sky, in the midst of which hung a reddish orb. *A red moon?* Lahlia had once said something about a "blood moon." The sky began to vibrate and rotate. It took several revolutions before Tucker realized that it was not the stars rotating, but the altar turning beneath him. The stone block was on a pivot, and the priests were turning it. He could hear their grunts of effort as they spun it faster and faster, like a flesh-and-stone version of spin the bottle. After a few more revolutions, the altar juddered to a stop.

He heard the deep voice of the bearded priest shout out a word: *"Bitte!"* Tucker was able to turn his head far enough to see the priest moving from one face of the pyramid to the next, stopping at each to call out to the murmuring crowd.

*"Bitte!"*

After the fifth call, the crowd fell into total silence.

The bearded priest walked up to Tucker and raised his right hand high over his head. Tucker saw the glint of torchlight on a shiny, black, wedge-shaped blade, and the strangely colored moon, and the harsh, angry features of the priest. The black blade flickered. He heard a grunt of effort and felt something slam into his chest. For a moment he thought he had only been punched, but when the priest withdrew the blade, it was followed by a bright red fountain of blood.

**23  THE FOREST**

THE SKY WAS BLUE, THE TREES WERE THICK WITH GREEN
needles and yellow leaves, and an incredibly old woman was
bending over Tucker. Her pale eyes, muted jade, searched
his face anxiously. Her hair was the color of cigarette ash. He
thought he had never seen anyone so ancient, but at the same
time she looked familiar, like the way he imagined his own
grandmother, whom he had never met.

The air smelled of pine needles, rotting leaves, and wood
smoke.

"Trackenspor? Septan? *Deutsch?*" The old woman pointed a
gnarled finger at her mouth. Behind her, a disk shimmered and
pulsed.

Tucker tried to speak, but something was squeezing his
chest, giving him barely enough slack to breathe. He moved his
head from side to side, saying no to whatever the woman was
asking.

*"Français? Non?"* She held a knobby walking stick in her right hand.

Tucker shook his head. He remembered the blood, and being lifted from the altar, and then a familiar inside-out, falling moment. He understood that he had been thrown through a disk but remembered nothing after that until he opened his eyes and found this strange old woman mouthing unintelligible questions at him.

*"¿Inglés?"* Her eyes widened; her pupils dilated. "English!" Her lips peeled back to reveal a collection of small, even teeth. It took Tucker a moment to recognize the expression as a smile.

*"¿Cómo está usted?"*

Tucker shook his head.

The old woman rapped herself on top of the head with her stick. "English, English! Too many tongues." She walked around him, using her walking stick but not seeming to really need it. "Leg coverings, the name, the name . . ." She pointed her stick at his legs. *"Pantas? Genus?"*

"Jeans," Tucker managed to whisper.

"Jeans! And . . . and a *blouson*? Blouse? Prenumerary? Digital?"

Tucker shook his head helplessly. He felt weirdly disconnected from his body. In his head, he was terrified; his heart should be pounding, but his body felt relaxed. He sensed only a steady, calm rhythm from within his chest.

"Your heart has been damaged." Her voice sounded more normal now. "The Lah Sept are efficient with their knives."

She rapped her stick against his chest. It made a dull clacking sound. Tucker lifted his head enough to see a convex metallic plate affixed to his chest.

"The cardiac support you are wearing is temporary." She scooped him into her arms, carrying him as if he weighed no more than an infant. "If you wish to live, you must tell me now. Live? Or die?"

"Live," Tucker croaked.

They climbed a low rise. A few yards to the side of the path, another disk hovered a few inches above the carpet of pine needles.

"I went . . . through," said Tucker, gesturing weakly as they passed the disk.

"The diskos, yes." The woman continued to walk.

Tucker drew in as much air as he was able, then said, "My dad . . . was . . . here?" The effort exhausted him.

"Do not speak," said the woman. She stopped walking and looked at him sharply. "What is your name?"

Tucker took two shallow breaths, then managed to squeeze out, "Tucker."

The woman slowly nodded her head. "Ah. Tucker Feye. I did not recognize you."

Tucker shook his head, not understanding.

"As the Boggsians say, 'What goes around comes around.'" She was walking again. "There is an ancient curse: 'May you live in interesting times.' You have heard it?"

Tucker shook his head again.

"It may postdate you. Welcome to the Terminus."

Tucker tried to reply, but he could not get enough air. The old woman frowned and began walking more quickly. "A Medicant disko is near," she said. "Do not die." Seconds later, they arrived at another disk, this one with its bottom edge resting upon the pine duff. Tucker's breathing had become shallower with each step. He felt himself fading.

"Do not be disturbed by their poor bedside manner," she said. "They cannot help themselves." She fed him into the disk.

# 24  THE HOSPITAL

THE DREAMS CAME AND WENT.

Swinging from the tree at Hardy Lake.

The acrid smell of burning jet fuel.

Torchlight reflecting off a black stone blade.

A girl with soft yellow hair and large dark eyes peering into his face. Tucker tried to sit up, but he could not move. "Lahlia?"

Lahlia's face morphed into that of his mother. "Mom?" He raised his arm, reaching out to her, but she stepped quickly back out of his reach and faded away.

Another dream followed: standing at a long table in a sea of identical tables, performing the same motions with his hands, again and again.

Tucker awakened in utter darkness.

Where was he? Back on the pyramid? No, the surface beneath him was too soft. Home in bed? The surface was not soft enough, and it did not smell like home. It smelled like . . . nothing. He opened and closed his mouth. No taste, good or bad.

Was he alive?

He sat up. A light came on. A featureless beige surface. A wall. He turned his head slowly from side to side. A small room, about eight feet on a side, no windows, one door, a small table attached to the side of the bed. No sheets or blankets, just a smooth, skinlike covering over the mattress.

It all looked strangely familiar.

He looked down at his body. A thin tube ran from the wall behind the bed into a plastic port embedded just above his navel. He was naked except for a pair of filmy shorts, and on his feet . . . From his ankles down they looked as if they had been dipped in thick, rubbery blue paint—the same sort of foot covering that his father and Lahlia had been wearing the day they arrived in Hopewell.

Lahlia. She had known what would happen to him—that the disk would land him on that pyramid. She had warned him about the priests. Tucker flipped through his memories, trying to sort dreams from reality. Had he really been stabbed? He examined his chest and found a jagged white scar that hadn't been there before. He also noticed several hairs growing around his nipples and across his chest. Chest hair? He sat up and eased himself off the bed. He felt fine—better than fine. He felt *strong*. The blue foot coverings were remarkably comfortable. He would have walked a few steps to try them out, but he was tethered to the wall by the tube in his belly.

Before he could figure out how to detach it, the door slid back. A bald man in gray coveralls stepped into the room. Several studs of varying colors were arranged in a grid on his chest, and he was wearing a complicated-looking headset with blue and yellow lights blinking over his left temple. He glared at Tucker, his mouth tight. Without saying a word, the man lifted him easily and set him back onto the bed.

"Hey!" Tucker said. The man pushed Tucker firmly back until he was lying on the thin mattress, then he touched one of the colored studs on his chest. Tucker felt himself sliding back into oblivion.

The next time Tucker woke up, the same man was running a palm-size plastic device over his abdomen, his hands covered with gloves of the same flesh-hugging blue plastic that coated Tucker's feet. The lights on his headset were blinking rapidly. Another man and a woman, heads shaved, wearing white coveralls, stood near the open door, watching. Both of them wore similar headsets, but without the blinking lights.

Tucker raised his head. "Where am I?" he asked.

The man ignored him.

"Can I have some clothes?"

No response.

"Are you a doctor?"

The man nodded curtly, then turned to the woman. "Nine eight six neurotypical," he said in oddly accented English.

The woman unfolded a small plastic tablet and typed rapidly with one hand.

"Nine eight six?" Tucker said. "Nine eight six what?"

The doctor produced a device that looked like an over-engineered screwdriver and touched it to the spot where the tube entered Tucker's body. Tucker lost all sensation below his rib cage. The doctor grasped the end of the tube, twisted, and pulled. Four inches of tubing came out of Tucker's abdomen with a sucking sound, leaving a hole behind. Tucker felt nothing. The doctor quickly placed a palm-size, flesh-colored patch over the wound. The patch melted and merged with Tucker's skin. A few seconds later, only a slight pucker marked where the hole had been.

The doctor said, "Twenty-two."

The woman held her tablet out. The doctor pressed his gloved thumb to one corner. The woman refolded the tablet and returned it to her pocket.

"Am I okay?" Tucker asked. Sensation was returning to his lower body. He felt no pain, but the spot where the tube had been began to itch.

"Nine eight six," the doctor said, frowning at Tucker as if to say, *Why are you wasting my time?*

"I don't understand," said Tucker.

The doctor shook his head disgustedly and snapped off his blue gloves. "Eighty-six," he said to the woman, and walked out of the room.

"I want my clothes," Tucker said.

The woman slid aside a panel in the wall and handed him a pair of gray coveralls.

"Where are *my* clothes?" he asked.

Wordlessly, she opened a second wall panel and produced his T-shirt, underwear, and jeans, all cleaned and carefully folded. Tucker quickly pulled on his underwear, which felt a bit snug, then his jeans. The jeans had shrunk—they were three inches too short, and he could barely get them buttoned. He gave the woman a puzzled look.

"What did you do? Boil them?"

The woman did not reply.

Tucker stepped out of the shrunken jeans and put on the coveralls. They fit him perfectly.

"What about my shoes?" he said, looking down at his blue feet.

She shook her head. The two orderlies—that was what Tucker had decided they were—took him by the arms and led him out of the beige room into a long gray hallway lined with beige doors.

"Where are you taking me?"

"Eighty-six," said the male orderly. They walked down the hallway, the male orderly's hand firmly on Tucker's back, urging him along. Many of the doors were open; Tucker caught glimpses into rooms exactly like the one he had occupied. In one room, a yellow-haired girl was lying on her back. Her face was bandaged, several tubes pierced her abdomen, and her legs were supported by a complex metal armature. Lahlia? Tucker stopped, but the orderly grabbed his arm and kept him moving on down the hall.

"Eighty-six!" said the orderly.

Tucker tried to pull away. The female orderly grasped his other arm; they lifted him so that his feet were a few inches off the ground and continued down the hallway, deaf to his protests. Tucker squirmed and tried kicking at their ankles, but his kicks had no effect.

At the end of the hallway, they entered a small cubicle and set him back on his feet. Tucker felt a pressure against the bottoms of his feet and realized they were in an elevator, going up. A few seconds later one wall slid back to reveal a flat, open rooftop overlooking a vast city. For a panicked moment, Tucker's mind flashed back to the Twin Towers — but this was not New York. These buildings all had a blocky sameness, and their colors were variations on the beige and gray of the hospital.

A hazy orange sun floated just above the horizon. Sunrise or sunset? He had no idea.

The orderlies turned away from the sun. A few yards in front of them stood a disk framed by a metal armature. The disk's edge just touched the pebbly gray surface of the roof.

The orderlies released him. "Go," said the woman, urging him toward the disk.

"Where does it go?" Tucker asked suspiciously.

The male orderly gave him a shove. *"Vamos,"* he said.

The surface of the disk abruptly changed texture and color, becoming grainy like a malfunctioning television, then pulsing bright green. The orderlies grabbed Tucker and pulled him away.

The disk hissed, gasped, and spat. A body wrapped in a cocoon of blood-spotted white fabric thumped onto the roof. A man. Long black hair, beard, dark skin, prominent eyebrows, and several deep, unhealed scratches on his forehead and cheeks. His brown eyes were open, unblinking, and dry. His lips had pulled back in a frozen grimace, revealing a set of large yellow teeth. He looked extremely dead.

The female orderly fingered her tablet urgently. Seconds later, four men emerged from the elevator with a floating gurney. They affixed a device that looked like an armored breastplate onto the dead man's chest, shoved a long tube down his throat, inserted a probe into his side, lifted him onto the gurney, and floated him into the elevator.

As soon as they were gone, the male orderly nudged Tucker toward the disk, which had returned to its previous cloudy shimmer.

*"Vamos."*

"Not until you tell me where it goes," Tucker said. He did not want to end up back on that pyramid—or worse.

"Home," said the woman.

"Home?" Tucker said.

The man gave Tucker a hard shove, sending him stumbling into the disk.

Not home.

The tangy, rich smell of autumn forest was overpowering after the sterile, odorless hospital. Tucker could feel the pine needles beneath his palms and hear the soft, mosquitolike buzz of the disk behind him. He crawled quickly away, putting a few yards between himself and the disk, then stood and looked around. His eyes adjusted. A full moon, low in the sky, filtered through the trees, casting weird shadows on all sides.

For several minutes he stood without moving, trying to sort things out. Had he been to the future? To some alternate universe? And what was *this* place? He remembered an old woman carrying him through a forest. This forest?

After a time, his thoughts stuttered and slowed. He noticed two faint moonlit paths leading away from the disk. He chose the one to the left and followed it.

# PART FOUR

# AWN

*A certain Theory of Revocable Causality came into vogue among a subcluster of the Klaatu. The Theory stated that alterations to past events would inevitably affect future events and that the further in the past the altera-tion occurred, the more profound would be the changes to the present. In other words, causing a Jurassic Period archosaur to flick its tail at the wrong moment might kill the ratlike proto-mammal that might have become the ancestor to* Homo sapiens.

*The faction embracing this theory became known as the Gnomon.*

*A vigorous debate ensued, including the following widely quoted exchange between the Gnomon Chayhim and the artist Iyl Rayn.*

*Chayhim: Damaging the established timestreams might preclude our very existence.*

*Iyl Rayn: The simple fact that you exist is sufficient to disprove your theory.*

*Chayhim: Iyl Rayn makes the assumption that our present state is more profound than that which we might have achieved had she not created the diskos. There is no proof of this. We believe we are greater than ourselves.*

*Iyl Rayn: You, sir, are a moron.*

*The Gnomon, unconvinced by Iyl Rayn's arguments, employed a team of Boggsian technicians to create a force of semi-intelligent cyberorganisms they called Timesweeps. These Timesweeps employed portable, self-contained diskos to travel through time and space. Their mission was to unwind the acts of corporeals who used the diskos and, having done so, to destroy the offending diskos so they could not be used again, much like an army burning bridges during a retreat.*

— $\mathbf{E}^3$

# 25 ARMA

On the morning after the escape of the Pure Girl Lah Lia and the subsequent sacrifice of the intruder who had interrupted the ritual, Brother Mynka, acolyte to Master Gheen, was on his hands and knees atop the Cydonian Pyramid using a short-bristle brush to scrub clean the stone surface of the frustum. He was rubbing out a particularly stubborn blood-stain when he was startled by a sharp popping sound.

Brother Mynka thought one of the torchères had fallen over, but when he looked up, he discovered a pinprick of orange luminescence dancing just above the surface of the altar stone. As he watched, the orange spark swelled into a fist-size sphere, then stretched itself horizontally to become a fat halo.

Brother Mynka dropped his brush and backed away until he reached the edge of the frustum. The halo-shaped light continued to expand, even as it appeared to be falling into itself. Brother Mynka gasped as understanding blossomed. He had been taught that such things existed, but he never imagined he would confront one in real life.

Only one creature grew larger as it consumed itself.

A *maggot.*

Brother Mynka watched the halo change color from orange to rose, shifting shape and growing until it became a bright pink segmented grub the size of an enormous hog. Definitely a maggot.

Both the maggot and Brother Mynka remained motionless for what seemed like a very long time. Finally, the maggot raised one end of its body. It had no visible eyes, but Brother Mynka detected a small orifice that might have been its mouth. It moved its head — if it was a head — in a slow, questing circle, pausing as it faced each of the Gates surrounding the frustum.

Brother Mynka willed himself to run, but his legs, paralyzed by a combination of fascination and terror, refused to obey.

The maggot paused facing Aleph, the most beneficent of the Gates. Its orifice expanded until it grew large enough to swallow a man. But the orifice was not a hole. It was a flat disk of swirling gray — a Gate.

The maggot's body slowly elongated, stretching from the altar stone across the frustum toward Aleph. By the time it reached Aleph, the maggot's orifice had expanded to match the Gate in size. It now looked like a long pink funnel, its small end anchored impossibly to the altar stone, its wide end suspended in midair. Aleph and the Gate within the maggot's orifice faced each other, separated by only the width of a hand. The space between them shimmered with orange light and emitted a low-pitched hum. Brother Mynka could feel the vibrations in his chest. The humming abruptly ceased and was followed by a sound like a dog slurping water.

The thing retracted slowly, returning to its original maggoty shape.

Brother Mynka gaped at the empty space, his heart beating wildly. Aleph, the Healing Gate, was gone.

Even through the terror of the moment, Brother Mynka fervently hoped that he would not be held responsible for losing Aleph. When things went wrong, Master Gheen was notorious for automatically punishing the nearest available acolyte.

Brother Mynka also hoped to avoid being devoured by the maggot. If only he could make his legs move. The maggot pulsed, a ripple ran along its body from tail to head, and Brother Mynka heard something that sounded like a belch.

The sound moved Brother Mynka beyond shock and fear; he regained control of his legs, stepped over the edge of the frustum, and bounded down the steep ledges at a speed just short of falling. He hit the zocalo at top speed and seconds later burst through the doors of the temple, shouting about giant, belching, Gate-eating worms. By the time Master Gheen strode forth from his study, Brother Mynka was surrounded by acolytes, all trying to make sense of his frightened babbling.

Master Gheen, admired and feared for his ability to make

instantaneous and irrevocable decisions, stepped through the crowd of excited acolytes and delivered a slap to Brother Mynka's left cheek.

It worked. Brother Mynka and the others fell instantly silent.

"Speak slowly," said Master Gheen.

Brother Mynka swallowed, staring into the harsh eyes of the head priest, and told them what he had witnessed.

Master Gheen's face became darker as he absorbed Brother Mynka's story. At the point when Brother Mynka was describing the maggot swallowing Aleph, Master Gheen turned abruptly and ran from the temple. Brother Mynka and the others followed. Master Gheen raced across the zocalo, his yellow robe flapping, then ascended the steep side of the pyramid at a speed that belied his years. Brother Mynka hesitated, then followed his master up the steps of the pyramid.

By the time Mynka reached the frustum, the maggot had swallowed Heid and was extending itself toward Gammel. Master Gheen was beating it furiously on the neck with his baton. The baton spouted an electrical charge with each blow but had no effect on the maggot. Brother Mynka, casting aside his fear, hammered with his fists at the thing's base. It was like hitting a solid block of oiled rubber.

Moments later, Gammel was gone.

Master Gheen stepped back and watched as the thing reformed itself into a plump maggot atop the altar stone and belched.

"It will rest, then eat again," said Brother Mynka.

Master Gheen gave him a venomous look, then ran to the edge of the frustum and shouted one word at the acolytes gathered at the base of the pyramid.

*"Arma!"*

Several of the acolytes ran off to the temple. Master Gheen turned his attention to Brother Mynka. "How did you cause this to happen?" he asked.

Brother Mynka shook his head helplessly, gesturing at his abandoned brush and the bucket of water. Master Gheen's face contorted; he drew back his charged baton and swung it against the side of Brother Mynka's neck. The acolyte collapsed on the frustum, muscles slack, eyes open, fully aware but unable to move. The Master struck him several more times with the baton, sending an agonizing jolt through his body with each blow. He then turned away and once again expended his fury on the maggot — which was beginning another elongation, this time in the direction of the Gate known as Dal — beating at it with such unrelenting fury that his baton began to smoke.

The acolyte Brother Koan arrived atop the frustum with the *arma,* a bright silver cylindrical device the same size as a baton. Brother Mynka had never seen an *arma* employed, but it was said to possess terrible power. Master Gheen grabbed the cylinder and shook it. The *arma* telescoped out to become a tapered tube the length of his arm.

The maggot's maw met Dal. Master Gheen aimed the silvery tube at the thing's midsection; a lance of eye-searing blue fire shot from its tip and sliced through the maggot. The mouth end of the beast instantly contracted and fell to the frustum with a splat. The tail end, still attached to the altar stone, shriveled into a knot of pink, smoldering meat.

The maggot had been destroyed, but too late. Dal had been swallowed. Only Bitte remained.

Master Gheen used the *arma* to obliterate the smoking remains of the maggot. He then pointed the tube at Brother Mynka.

"Prepare yourself," he said.

Brother Mynka closed his eyes for the last time.

# 26  NUMBERING THE DAYS

The paths through the woods faded in and out like deer trails. Tucker passed several of the strange disks before he realized that he had been walking in a circle. He slowed, watching the path more carefully. The moon was setting; the first light of dawn had turned the eastern sky a soft blue. Tucker came to a fork in the path he had not noticed before. He followed it to the left, up a steep hillside, and along a ridge, passing two more disks.

The path led down the right side of the ridge and onto an open, grassy meadow. At the far end of the meadow was a small cabin made of rough-hewn wooden planks. A yellow light shone from one of two windows.

Tucker hesitated at the edge of the forest, considering his choices. He could walk up to the cabin and knock on the door and see who answered. He could return to the disk that led to the hospital roof. Or he could enter one of the other disks and end up . . . somewhere.

What would his father do? What had his father *done*? Tucker knew his dad had survived the episode on the pyramid, because he had managed to return home, with Lahlia. Both of them must have also been to the hospital place, because they had been wearing those blue foot coverings when they arrived in Hopewell.

Tucker now thought he understood why his dad had taken his mom through the disk. He had gone to find a cure for her illness at that futuristic hospital. But that meant they would have to go back to the pyramid . . . or did it? Lahlia had told him there was a second "gate" in Hopewell. Or maybe each time you used them, the disks went to different places, or different times, the way the disk on the World Trade Center had returned him and Kosh to the same barn, but ten years apart.

Tucker sat on a fallen tree trunk and stared across the meadow. He didn't know enough to know what to do. The sky slowly brightened, bringing out the green and gold colors of the tall grasses. He could see no movement within the cabin, but after a time, a curl of smoke issued from the stone chimney.

He imagined knocking on the cabin door. The door would open and it would be . . . his mom! Smiling, sane, with a full head of red hair. "We've been waiting for you!" she would say. "Are you hungry?"

The fantasy produced a wave of warmth and hope; Tucker

let himself enjoy it for a few seconds, then brought himself back to reality. He *was* hungry. The last time he remembered eating was in Hopewell. A peanut-butter-and-pickle sandwich. He remembered the tube in his abdomen and guessed that it had carried food to his stomach. He swallowed. The thought of real food was making him salivate. Whoever was in the cabin might be able to feed him.

The chittering and tweeting of birds and other small creatures, hardly noticed by him before, increased tenfold as the first rays of sunlight flicked through the trees. Decisions impossible at night are more easily made at sunrise. Tucker walked through meadow grasses toward the cabin. He smelled wood smoke, then the aroma of something cooking. He did not have to knock. The door opened before he reached the porch. An old woman stepped out—the same ancient but vigorous woman who had carried him through the forest and sent him to the hospital. She was wearing a sleeveless calf-length shift the color and texture of wet sand. Her feet were bare.

"You're back," she said. "Are you hungry?"

"My name is Awn," said the old woman as she ladled what looked like oatmeal from a heavy iron pot into his bowl. "The people who sent you here are known as the Medicants."

"Medicants?"

"That is what they call themselves. A people driven by digital technologies and constrained by their societal ethic. It makes them resentful, particularly when the injured and the dead are thrust upon them."

"What is a societal ethic?" Tucker asked.

Awn served herself a ladle of the hot cereal and sat across from him at the trestle table.

"They have a mandate to cure the sick and injured."

"Could they cure autism?"

Awn stared into space for a few seconds, then said, "Autism. The naturalistic form of Plague." She shook her head. "The Medicants would not attempt to undo a condition they regard as optimal. However, they might implant digital sensory filters and enhancement devices such as they use upon themselves."

"Are you saying the Medicants are autistic?"

"In a sense. They carry Plague."

"But they can't cure themselves?"

"They choose to remain who they are. In any case, they would have to remove and regrow large portions of the brain. The result would be uncertain, and the cost would be steep. The Medicants are nothing if not miserly. How did you pay them for your own treatment?"

Tucker tasted his cereal. It wasn't oatmeal, but it tasted good.

"They didn't charge me," he said.

Awn looked at him. With her ash-colored hair and translucent, finely wrinkled skin she could have been a hundred years old, but her voice was strong and her eyes missed nothing.

"Whether you know it or not, you paid them," she said.

"You are alive, and they have given you a pair of Medicant boots."

Tucker looked down at his blue foot coverings. He had forgotten all about them.

"Do they come off?" He reached down and peeled back the top edge.

"Once you remove them they are useless to you. Wear them. They will carry you far. Now eat."

Tucker spooned warm cereal into his mouth. The more he ate, the better it tasted.

"Slow down," said Awn. "You have not eaten solid food in quite some time. You will make yourself sick."

Tucker set down his spoon. "How long was I in the hospital?"

"Long."

"Like a week?"

Awn stood, walked to the far corner of the room, lifted a small mirror from a hook on the wall, brought it back to the table, and held it up so Tucker could see himself.

The boy in the mirror was not him.

Rather, it *was* him, but not the Tucker Feye he knew. The Tucker in the mirror had a narrower face, longer hair, and a scanty but definite beard.

He ran his hand over his face, feeling the soft, unfamiliar whiskers.

Awn, watching him, nodded.

"A long time," she said, setting the mirror aside.

"I look old!"

"*I* look old. You are simply older than you were."

"Yeah, like sixteen! Or seventeen!"

Awn waved her hands in front of her face as if to fend off a bad smell.

"What?" Tucker was not sure what he had done. "How many years was I there?"

"We do not number the years," she said. "Eat."

Tucker ate another spoonful of cereal.

"What is this stuff?" he asked.

"Rolled spelt."

"Spelt?"

"A type of wheat."

"Oh. It's good." He chose his next words carefully. "What exactly happened to me?"

"You were injured. Dying. I sent you to the Medicants. They repaired the damage to your heart, and they took their fee."

"What fee?"

"Sometimes they take organs."

"You mean they took a kidney or something?"

"I do not think so. In your case, I think they took a portion of your life."

"I don't get it."

"Let me see your hands."

Tucker held out his hands; Awn held them gently, feeling each of his fingers.

"Your skin is thick and hard here . . . and here." She indicated a ridge of thickened flesh along each of the thumbs, and on his index fingers.

Tucker stared at the unfamiliar calluses. "What does it mean?"

"If you try, you might remember."

"I don't remember anything."

"The Medicants will have suppressed portions of your memory. They think it a kindness. Your mind, however, retains more than they know."

Tucker pulled his hands away. A panicky feeling rose from his gut. Too much had happened, and too quickly — the pyramid, the knife, the dreams — and now he was sitting in a cabin surrounded by a forest full of strange portals with an old lady looking at him as if he were a lab rat.

"You should rest," she said.

"I'm not tired. Why don't you tell me what this place is? Where are we?"

"This is the Terminus."

"Terminus?"

"The endpoint of the diskos."

"Diskos?"

"The means by which you arrived here."

"But where is 'here'?"

Awn stood and picked up her stick. "Come."

Tucker followed her outside onto the porch. The sun had risen above the trees; a faint mist hung over the meadow. Awn sat on one of two wooden chairs and directed Tucker to the other.

"We are alone here. The forest extends far in every direction. You could walk day and night, night and day, and you would find no others."

"Yeah, but where are we? I mean, is this even the United States?"

"Geographically, this place was once known as Hopewell County, Minnesota. But that was very long ago."

"You mean we're in the future? Like those Medicant people?"

"The time of the Medicants is long gone."

"Like the pyramid people?"

"The Lah Sept came to power after the Medicants, at the end of the Digital Age, but still, it was long ago."

"How far in the future is this?"

"This is the true present. The diskos do not yet exist beyond this moment."

"But what *year* is it?"

"I do not number the years."

"You don't know how long it's been?"

"Been since what?"

"Since . . . I don't know . . . since the Hopewell where I grew up."

"Is it so important to you?"

"Yes!"

Awn nodded and began to tap her walking stick on the wooden porch deck — *thump, thump, thump . . .*

"What are you doing?" he asked.

"I am tapping the seasons," said Awn, still tapping. "Fall, winter, spring . . ."

"Why?"

"You asked me how long it has been."

Tucker watched the stick go up and down with metronome regularity.

"I lost count."

"Do not *count.*" *Thump, thump* . . . "This will take some time. Are you not tired?"

He *was* tired. He had walked through the woods for . . . how long? Hours? And that rhythmic tapping. . . .

"There is a room, with a comfortable bed. Why don't you rest? We can talk more when you awaken."

Tucker could hardly hold his head up — he wondered if he was being hypnotized, but could not rouse himself enough to care. He managed to ask, "How do I know I won't fall asleep and wake up an old man?"

Awn nodded seriously. "Sometimes I feel that is what happened to me. I turned around three times and discovered myself as I am." Still tapping, she laughed at his expression. "Go. Rest. I do not exact blood for porridge."

Tucker thought he might just lie down for a few minutes. He needed to think, to order the questions whirling through his mind. He went inside. There were only two rooms in the small cabin: one main room and a smaller room with a bed. He lay down on the thin mattress.

The regular sound of wood striking wood continued.

Tucker slept.

# 27  CALCULATIONS

A NARROW TABLE EXTENDED AS FAR AS TUCKER COULD see, in both directions. It held a large number of gray plastic objects that looked like palm-size clamshells, each one filled with complicated-looking circuitry. The devices moved slowly along the table from left to right, propelled by some invisible force. As each clamshell reached Tucker's position he took a small gray piece of plastic from a tray at his elbow and snapped it into the circuitry. With each snap came a small jolt of pleasure.

Tucker was not the only person standing at the table. Every few feet, another man, woman, or child stood ready to add his or her own modification to the device. All were tethered to their stations by tubes leading from a port just above their navels to identical ports along the edge of the table.

Tucker snapped another widget into place, felt a familiar, satisfying bump of joy, then waited for the next incomplete clamshell to arrive, counting his heartbeats. *Thump-thump. Thump-thump. Thump-thump. Thump*—

Tucker opened his eyes. He could just make out the shapes of rough-hewn rafters in the near-dark. He was in Awn's cabin.

*Thump, thump, thump, thump, thump. . . .*

He had been dreaming, but the thumping was real. He sat up on the edge of the bed, blinking sleepily at the crude wooden walls. He felt as if he had slept for hours.

*Thump, thump, thump . . .*

Tucker stood and walked out of the bedroom. A flickering lantern above the woodstove illuminated the main room. The window and open doorway were dark. Had he slept all through the day and into the night? He looked at himself in the mirror hanging on the wall, felt his soft, scruffy beard.

He walked to the doorway. Moonlight flooded the meadow. Awn was sitting in her chair, thumping her walking stick, her eyes gazing out over the meadow. The tip of the stick had worn a depression half an inch deep in the soft wood of the porch floor.

"Have you been doing that all day?" Tucker asked.

Awn smiled and looked up at him. "Sit."

Tucker sat in the other chair. *Tapping out the seasons,* she had said. And how many seasons could she "tap out" in a day? He tried to add up the numbers. Two taps a second, sixty seconds per minute, sixty minutes per hour . . . That was about, what? About seventy-two hundred? Seventy-two hundred seasons would be eighteen hundred years for every hour . . . and she'd been tapping for at least five hours. Nine thousand years? And she was still tapping.

"Your calculations cause me discomfort," said Awn.

"You can tell what I'm thinking?"

"Your eyes cloud with numbers. Do not measure the time. Feel it." She continued to tap.

"You can stop," Tucker said.

"Are you certain?"

Tucker nodded.

Awn raised the stick and rested it across her lap. "Did you dream?"

Tucker told her about the table and the widgets. "I think I've dreamed the same dream before."

"Dreams are assembled from fragments of memory," Awn said. "That was a Medicant factory. They used you well."

"They had me working in their factory the whole time?"

"The Medicants do nothing for free."

Tucker ran his hand over his jaw, fascinated by its furry texture. A sadness came over him for his lost years. He wondered again, How long? A year? Two? Five? He might never know his true age.

"You are fortunate," said Awn, "that they did not take more."

That night, over a meal of bean stew, black bread, and braised parsnips, Tucker talked with Awn about his parents. "I'm pretty sure they went through the disko that goes to the—what did you call the pyramid people? The Lah something?"

"The Lah Sept," said Awn. "Eat."

Tucker ate another spoonful of the stew, then said, "I'm pretty sure they went into the disk—the disko—and that landed them on top of that pyramid—"

"The Cydonian Pyramid," said Awn. "You were on the frustum."

"Frustum?"

"A frustum is the flat top of a pyramid. Is that not an English word?"

"I never heard it before. Anyway, I think my dad took my mom there to get her to the Medicants. Because she was sick."

Awn nodded.

"So did they have to come *here* to get *there*?"

"People come; people go."

"I have to find them." Tucker sat back in his chair. "How do I do that?"

"I do not know."

"These disko things. Do they always take you to the same place?"

"Yes," said Awn. "And no."

"Thanks a lot."

Awn shrugged. "Wherever you go, there you are. Poorly phrased questions produce unsatisfactory responses."

"But I—"

"Eat your beans. Your questions will wait for tomorrow."

\* \* \*

With Awn refusing to answer any more questions, Tucker retired to the porch, where he sat staring out into the night, listening to the babble of the tree frogs and crickets, the sounds of night. Under the full moon, the meadow grasses became a fibrous ocean of icy silver and pale gold. His thoughts whirled. What did he know? He was in some distant future, if Awn's tapping was to be believed. He had access to the diskos. He was free to go if he wished. He could walk out into the woods at any time, choose a disko, and travel to another place.

Did he *want* to leave? So far, Awn had shown no inclination to plunge a knife into him or turn him into a factory zombie. All she had done was feed him, offer him shelter, and dispense a few paltry bits of information. For the moment, he felt safe.

He could hear her stirring inside: the clink of metal on metal, scraping, the creak of a pump handle, the sound of water splashing into the basin. Should he have offered to help with the dishes? She had not seemed to expect it. He wondered again what she was doing here in this cabin and why she knew so much about the disks—diskos, portals, whatever—and why all her answers to his questions simply led to more questions. And what was her deal with numbers? How crazy would a person have to be to spend a whole day pounding a stick on the floor rather than just saying, *Nine thousand years*—or whatever the number would have come to if she had kept on tapping.

Nine thousand *years*! The thought made him feel hollow and unreal—and what sort of person could tap a stick for hours and hours without getting tired? He remembered his nightmarish journey from the pyramid to the hospital of the Medicants. Awn had picked him up and carried him through the woods. The old woman looked like ninety pounds of wrinkles and bone, hardly strong enough to lift a child.

Maybe this was some sort of virtual reality and he was strapped to a machine and someone was feeding dreams into his brain. That thought brought him a weird sort of comfort, although he did not believe it for a moment. Breathing in the pine-scented air, feeling the rough boards beneath his feet, he knew to the bottom of his soul that this cabin, this place, was utterly real.

Awn came out of the cabin and, without looking at him, stepped off the porch and walked out into the meadow. The grasses came up to her waist. She stopped midway across and stood without moving for several seconds.

Tucker heard what sounded like men's voices filtering through the trees, calling out in some strange tongue. Awn quickly crossed the far side of the meadow and disappeared into the woods. Tucker waited a few seconds, then followed her. As he reached the edge of the field he heard more shouting, and then a hoarse scream followed by a bright-orange flash from far back in the trees. The voices ceased abruptly. He stood still, listening as the night creatures gradually resumed their babble. He took a few steps toward where the sounds had come from, but he had missed the path and quickly became disoriented. After a long quarter hour of crashing through the underbrush, he found himself back in the meadow.

A pale shape—Awn—emerged from the trees a few yards away.

"Tucker Feye. Are you lost?"

"I heard voices," he said.

"They come; they go. It is time to rest." They crossed the meadow to the cabin, Awn using her stick and moving more slowly than usual.

"Who was that?" Tucker asked as they stepped up onto the porch.

"No one you would know." She went inside.

Tucker stood for a few moments on the porch, trying unsuccessfully to make sense of his situation, then followed her inside. Awn was sitting at the table, motionless, staring into space.

"Awn?"

She did not reply. She did not seem to know he was there. Tucker waved his hand in front of her face, but got no response. Not even a blink.

He sat with her until his eyes would no longer stay open, then took himself to the other room and sank onto the bed.

That night he dreamed of a long hallway lined with gray doors. The Medicant hospital. One of the doors slid open. Lahlia was sitting on the bed wearing the silver shift and blue boots she had worn during her first visit to Hopewell. She stared back at him with her dark eyes. He tried to ask her about his father, but when he opened his mouth nothing came out. Suddenly he was back in the hallway and all the doors were closed. He ran from door to door, pounding with his fists, certain that behind one of them he would find his parents.

## 28  THE KLAATU DISKOS

TUCKER AWAKENED AT DAWN. RUBBING HIS EYES, HE walked into the main room. Awn was stirring something on the stove.

"Good morning," he said.

Awn nodded, lifted the heavy iron pot from the stove, and carried it to the table with no apparent effort.

"You're a lot stronger than you look," Tucker said.

"I am no stronger than you," she said.

"I don't think I could pick me up and carry me the way you did."

"You may be surprised by what you are capable of doing." She ladled hot spelt into the bowls.

"Did you sleep?" Tucker asked.

"I am rested. Eat your breakfast."

Tucker ate, planning his next request for information. He worked his way through the bowl of spelt, composing and rejecting questions. When he finally spoke, the question that popped out was not the one he'd meant to ask.

"Am I dead?"

"Yes," said Awn.

Tucker stared at her in shock.

"But not here," she added. "Not now."

Tucker relaxed — slightly.

"Your question is casuistic," Awn said.

"Huh?"

"Am I using the wrong language?"

"I don't know what that word — ca-zoo-whatever."

"Your question is not answerable in its present form. Time is not symmetrical. You cannot uneat your spelt, yet the uneaten spelt exists in the recent past. You will die — in a sense you are already dead — but you are not dead in the here and now."

"You know when I'm going to die?"

"You will live the life you will live. Is that not sufficient?"

"Um, not really."

Awn stood up. "Come. I will give you a tour of the diskos."

"They are fickle," said Awn. She stopped walking and thrust her stick into a disko. The surface pulsed and formed a whirlpool around the stick's point of entry. "This one leads to the site of the assassination of a politician, but rarely to the assassination event itself."

"Why doesn't it suck in the stick?" Tucker asked, standing

several feet back from the disko. "Every time I got that close to one it sucked me up like a vacuum cleaner."

"They find you more interesting than they do me."

"You mean . . . like, they're alive?"

"Not in the sense you mean." She withdrew her stick from the whorl. "But they are attracted to those who can perceive them. Most corporeals are blind to the diskos and are therefore not drawn to them."

"Do you mean some people can't go through?"

"Anyone may be transported, but some must forcibly encounter the field. As you have seen, most diskos are located inconveniently, where the unwary are not apt to stumble into them. Except here at the Terminus, of course."

"Why is here different?"

Awn ignored the question. "Few of the Lah Sept, for example, can see the diskos."

"But there were thousands of—" Tucker stopped when Awn winced at his use of *thousands*. "I mean, there was a whole plaza full of people watching when I was on that pyramid. They couldn't see the diskos?"

"Of the Lah Sept, only the priests, the Yars, and others who have received training actually *see* them. The sacrifices are hurled from the edge of the pyramid into a disko, but the people on the zocalo see only a flash of orange. Though they imagine more."

"How come I can see them?"

"As I said, they find you interesting." She gestured at the disko with her stick. "The reverse side of this would take you to France during the bubonic plague, a destination popular with the Klaatu."

"Klaatu?" Lahlia had called the ghosts Klaatu. "Are they like . . . dead people?"

"They are not dead. Nor are they alive, in the usual sense."

"Why are they called Klaatu?"

"The inventor of the technology that allowed them to transcend the physical was a connoisseur of ancient video projections."

"You mean movies?"

"Yes." Awn resumed walking, her pace as regular as a metronome. Tucker followed her to a disko hovering over a mossy boulder.

"This disko leads to a place called Auschwitz, where many were killed with terrible efficiency." She walked around the boulder to the other side of the disko. "This side I do not know. Another attempted genocide, perhaps. Come." She followed a faint path through a patch of gooseberry bushes and stopped before another disko that seemed to rest on its edge beneath the sagging branches of a white pine. "This is the disko where I found you. It leads to the Cydonian Pyramid in the city of Romelas near the end of the reign of the Lah Sept priesthood. You are fortunate that I was nearby when you were cast through. The other side also leads to Romelas, but to a later point in that city's history. Pure Girls who survive the frustum often choose to return home by this route."

"Lahlia said she was a Pure Girl," Tucker said, more to himself than to Awn.

Awn tipped her head as if consulting an inner voice. She nodded. "The Yar Lia, yes."

"Lahlia was here?"

"She called herself Yar Lia. She and many others have passed through the Terminus. Come. We have far to go."

The next disko stood at the crest of a hill.

"I once saw a large red-and-blue parrot fly squawking from this disko," Awn said. "It did not survive the winter. I have seen other tropical birds in the forest; they may have come from here as well. Entering from the opposite side of this disko would take you to the landing of the Viking spacecraft on Mars."

"Mars the planet?"

"Yes. You would not wish to go there in your corporeal state."

"How come there's a disko there?"

"So that the Klaatu might witness the Martian tragedy. It was before your time, yes? You would not have known. The Viking spacecraft infected the Martian ecosystem with terrestrial prions and other organic matter. Biocide on a planetary scale. Generations passed before anyone realized that Mars had once supported life, and that the entire Martian biota had been infected and destroyed as a result of human trespass. Come."

Awn led Tucker down a steep path to the edge of a tamarack swamp, where three diskos hung a few feet above the peaty soil. Two transparent figures, a man and a woman, hovered before the middle disk. They were looking right at Tucker.

"Are those Klaatu?"

"Yes. You fascinate them," said Awn. She swept her stick through the two figures. They broke into shards of mist, then dissipated. "They have abandoned their corporeal existence, yet they retain consciousness without measurable physical presence."

"But I can see them. Isn't that physical?"

"No. The Klaatu are composed of information. You become aware of them through other means, then your mind constructs an appropriate image. There is no actual *seeing* involved."

A male Klaatu swam out of the central disko. Awn poked at it with her stick. The Klaatu broke apart.

"When you do that, are you killing them?" Tucker asked.

"I am merely disrupting our awareness of them. It amuses me." Awn pointed at the left-hand disko. "The Krakatoa explosion, observed from a ship in the Sunda Strait. You would not survive." She pointed at the other disko. "A cavern in Gibraltar where the last true Neanderthals were slaughtered by their Cro-Magnon neighbors."

"How come practically every one of these disko things leads to something awful?"

"The Klaatu are fascinated by the terrible, the horrific, the irreversible. Because the Klaatu are, in a sense, already dead, they are endlessly fascinated by the true deaths of others. Their fear of what they are is what drives them to use the diskos. They devote themselves exclusively to their own self-absorption, and it is for this that they are ashamed. Shame was what ultimately led Klaatu known as the Gnomon to declare the diskos morbid and atavistic—even as other Klaatu continued to access them."

"Who made the diskos?"

"The diskos were constructed by Boggsians under the guidance of a Klaatu artist known as Iyl Rayn."

"What's a Boggsian?" Tucker imagined something with eight legs and sharp claws.

"The Boggsians supply digital technology to anyone who will pay, though they eschew such technologies for their own use. You will meet them one day. Recognize them by their beards and black hats—they are the descendants of Amish Jews."

Tucker said, "Amish Jews? Aren't the Amish and Jews complete opposites?"

"The sonnets of Shakespeare have yet to be typed by a monkey, yet stranger things have occurred." With that cryptic comment, Awn continued on down the path. Tucker shook his head and followed. As they entered a boggy grove of soft-needled, moss-draped tamarack trees, Tucker heard a crunching and splashing in the distance. He looked through the trees and saw a man wearing a red jerkin and a metal helmet, leaping from hummock to hummock, running like a frightened deer.

"Who was that?" Tucker asked.

"He is lost. Do not worry; he will find his way. Come."

She continued along the path. Tucker noticed that Awn never slowed or stumbled.

They came to a disk jutting up through a pool of stagnant water. Only about a third of it was visible. "This one emits snakes and lizards," Awn said. "They do not survive here for long, which makes me think the reverse would be true as well."

"Don't any of these things go to someplace normal?"

"There is no normal."

"I mean normal like Hopewell, where people aren't getting killed and things aren't exploding and stuff."

"The diskos lead to interesting times, as defined by their designer."

"So, can I get home from here?"

"Yes," said Awn. "And no." She continued along the path. Tucker followed.

"I wish you wouldn't do that," he said.

"Do what?"

"That 'yes . . . and no' thing."

Awn laughed. "As I have told you, this *is* Hopewell. In a sense you are already home."

"I want to go back to *my* Hopewell."

"There is no direct route from here to your Hopewell."

"I can't get there from here?"

"You could return the way you arrived."

Tucker thought back to his brief and violent moments atop the pyramid. Even if he could get past the priests, he did not think he would be able to tell which of the five diskos had brought him from Hopewell.

"That's the only way?"

"There are others."

"Is any way not dangerous?"

"No."

"So, every one of these things goes to someplace where I might get killed?"

"I did not say that."

"What should I do?" he asked.

"There is no *should*."

"I can't just stay here forever."

Awn stopped and pointed her walking stick at Tucker's chest. "You must gather information. When you feel you are ready, you select a disko and leave this place. It is what everyone does, even that man we just saw. You learn and you choose. Choose well, and you may find yourself where you wish to be."

"You said the diskos always lead to the same places, but what about when you go back through? Do you always end up where you started?"

"Reentering a disko will often return you to your approximate geographical point of origin, though not always. If you were to return to the Cydonian Pyramid, you would likely find yourself facing the same priests, who would attempt to kill you again. Or you might arrive somewhat later. Others entering the same disko might be taken to a different time, or even a different place. The diskos are an instrument, like those—what do you call them?" Awn held out her hands and wiggled her fingers.

"Pianos?" Tucker said.

"No. The things in your places of worship."

"Like in a church? You mean like an organ?"

"Yes! An organ, with its pipes and stops and bellows and moans. They open and close and change in pitch and volume."

"You mean somebody is playing the diskos? Like an instrument?"

"Yes and no. Once, perhaps, but then not." She shook her head. "Language is inadequate. They are not played, exactly. Imagine the organ as a collection of willful beasts, pulling in different directions. A closed system containing infinite variations."

"I'm sorry I asked," said Tucker, more confused than before.

They continued through the bog. Awn pointed out a disko that she said led to two historical events that meant nothing to Tucker—the murder of a Detroit labor organizer named Jimmy Hoffa, and the rupture of the Glen Canyon Dam.

They climbed a short, steep path onto a piney ridge.

Tucker said, "How many—I mean, there sure are a lot of diskos here."

"Yes." Awn stopped before another disko. On the ground was the hilt end of a broken sword and a worn leather scabbard. The pine needles were trampled and stained by a large quantity of what appeared to be dried blood.

"I heard men shouting last night," Tucker said.

Awn did not reply.

"Where does this one go?" he asked.

"The death of a prophet."

As Tucker examined the disko, he noticed something half-buried in the pine duff. Tucker's heart swelled and pounded as he picked it up. It was the same hand-carved wooden troll he had once wedged into a toy fire truck and catapulted onto the roof of their house.

**29   PRIESTS**

"My dad carved this," Tucker said, holding up the troll. "He was here!"

"Perhaps so." Awn looked at the broken sword. "Others as well."

"So does that mean he went into that thing?" He pointed at the disko. "Or did he come out of it?"

"I do not know," said Awn.

"You said this one goes to 'the death of a prophet.' What does that mean?"

Awn was already walking away. He started after her, then stopped and returned the troll to its place so he could find the disko again. He ran to catch up with her.

"All your questions will be answered in time," she said.

"Yeah, but—"

"Let us finish our tour. Tonight we will talk more."

They walked for more than two hours and visited dozens of diskos. Awn's slow, steady pace never varied, and she did not seem to tire; Tucker was exhausted both by the walking and by her always bewildering answers to his questions.

When at last they returned to the cabin, Tucker, wobbly in the legs and dizzy with information, retired to the bedroom and stared at the ceiling, trying to sort things out.

*You learn and you choose,* Awn had said. Easy to say. Not so easy to do.

Tucker thought of the wooden troll. Had his father left it as a signpost? Was it an invitation or a warning? Had he placed the troll there upon entering the disko or after he had emerged from it? And what lay on the other side?

*The death of a prophet,* Awn had said.

The smell of cooking wafted through the cabin. Tucker realized that he was famished. He got up and went into the main room just in time to see Awn leave through the front door. He followed her out onto the porch and stopped dead.

On the other side of the field, two yellow-robed, hooded figures emerged from the trees. Lah Sept priests. They saw Awn walking toward them and stopped. One of the priests pushed back his hood to reveal a shaved head and a scraggly beard. It was the priest who had stabbed him. Tucker moved back into the cabin and watched them from the shadows, his heart pounding.

Awn met them in the middle of the field. The head priest was gesturing with his hands and talking loudly in their strange tongue. Awn replied in the same language. Tucker could hardly breathe—was she *friends* with them?

The bearded priest became more agitated, raising his voice, while Awn made soothing gestures and spoke quietly.

The priest abruptly walked past her, coming straight for the cabin. Awn grasped his sleeve. The priest stopped and uttered a sharp command to his companion. The hooded priest pulled a short, black baton from within his robe and jabbed it at Awn's back. The device made a loud snapping sound. Awn's body convulsed; she spun and swung her walking stick at the man's wrist, knocking the weapon from his grasp. She said something to him, then turned away. The priest jumped on her back and threw one arm around her neck. Awn whipped her walking stick up and back, striking him on the head; the priest fell, stunned, to the grass. The bearded priest reached into his robes and came out with a bright-silver object. With a snap of his wrist, the device telescoped into a tube about a yard long. Awn, seeing what the priest held, moved sideways faster than any human should be able to move.

A ragged, eye-searing jet of energy crackled from the end of the tube, ripping through grass and earth as the priest swung it from right to left, leaving behind a charred, smoking scar. Awn dove beneath the beam, rolled, regained her feet, and ran at the priest, who brought the beam back, this time sweeping it across the old woman's midsection.

The sound was that of meat hitting a superheated grill. For a moment, Tucker thought Awn would be okay, that she would shrug it off as she had the discharge from the other priest's baton, but his hope crumbled in an instant as the two halves of Awn's body fell to the blackened grass.

Tucker felt as if he had been cut in half, too—one foot caught in a horrible nightmare, the other mired in an impossible reality. He stepped out the doorway and started toward them, then froze. What could he do?

The priest retracted his weapon and stood staring down at Awn's sundered and smoking remains. The second priest, recovering from the blow to his head, climbed to his feet and joined him. For several seconds, the priests stood side by side, their heads bowed. Tucker had the impression that they were praying. As if on cue, both turned their heads and looked toward the cabin, where Tucker stood in full view, framed by the doorway.

For a long, frozen moment, no one moved. The priests started walking, then running toward him, their robes billowing. Tucker felt as if he were stuck in slow time—he could not will himself to move. The head priest triggered his device again, and the door frame shattered inches above Tucker's head. That was enough to get him moving. He ran down the porch, around the back of the cabin, and toward the trees. As he entered the woods a tree trunk just to his left exploded. Tucker ducked his head and ran. He scrambled up a low ridge and down into a creek bed. The priests were shouting to each other—by their voices, he could tell they were spreading out. He splashed across the creek and ran between two closely spaced diskos and into a cedar swamp, trying to stay on the hummocks, leaping over fallen, rotting logs, ducking under low-hanging vines, a few times breaking through the mossy, boggy soil and plunging his leg into a sinkhole. He reached a rocky outcropping—the end of another piney ridge. He climbed up onto the ridge and stopped, gasping for breath. He could still hear them. A wet, crunching sound came from below; he caught a glimpse of yellow through the trees. Following the far side of the ridge, he kept moving, running, then stopping from time to time to catch his breath and listen. He followed the ridge as it curved to the right.

After a time—twenty minutes? an hour?—he reached the base of a steep, flat hillside. Only a few stunted trees were growing on the hill; the rest of it was covered with grasses. Tucker stopped to listen again, hearing only the rustling of the wind in the trees and an occasional birdcall.

He had lost them. For now. But he had lost himself as well. After all the zigging and zagging, he was completely disoriented. Thinking he might be able to see more from higher up, he climbed the steep hillside, using the little trees for handholds. Halfway up, the grass gave way to a giant stairway of waist-high, weathered, mossy stone blocks. The ruins of an ancient building? He climbed until he reached the top, a flat platform paved in lichen-covered stone, littered with leaves and pine needles, and crowded on every side by tree branches. He had hoped to see out over the top of the forest, but the platform was only about fifty feet above the ground.

Tucker crossed the platform and found another set of giant

steps leading down. His heart sped as realization struck. He circled the perimeter of the platform, finding three more steep, crumbling stairways. He was standing upon the ruins of the Cydonian Pyramid, or a very similar structure. He saw no diskos. Hearing a familiar buzzing sound, he looked straight up. Thirty feet above him was a single disko, flickering in the sunlight. Anybody coming out of that one would have a long drop.

If this was the same pyramid, it had aged thousands — maybe tens of thousands — of years. Over the millennia, it had settled into the earth; half of it was now buried beneath the forest floor.

And if this forest was, as Awn claimed, the Hopewell of the future, then that meant that the pyramid had been built in his own hometown. That thought sent a chill deep into Tucker's gut; he climbed down, skidding and sliding bumpily over the eroded steps, needing to put some distance between himself and the place where the stone blade had pierced his heart, and also thinking that this ruin might well attract the interest of the priests. He did not want to meet them on the pyramid again.

He continued walking, following the deer paths that twisted and coiled through the forest, keeping a close watch for the yellow-robed priests. There had to be someone somewhere. Another cabin. Another friendly old woman. He found a blackberry bush heavy with fruit and ate several handfuls, then discovered a small spring bubbling from a rocky slope and drank deeply; the water was sweet and crisp.

The sun had dropped below the treetops when he came

upon the top half of a disko jutting from a stagnant pool—the disko that Awn had said produced snakes and lizards. He had circled back—Awn's cabin was only a short distance away. The cabin was a source of food and shelter, but the priests might be waiting for him. He thought for a moment. If the priests were there, he could simply leave and be no worse off than before.

Retracing his steps from the day before, he reached the edge of the field. He could see the two halves of Awn's ruined body in the meadow. Tucker concealed himself behind a copse of hazelnut bushes and watched the cabin. For many minutes he saw no signs of activity, but after a time he heard voices. A priest stepped out of the woods about fifty yards from his hiding place and crossed the open area to the cabin, where he was greeted by the bearded priest, who had been waiting inside. Tucker held his breath. Slowly, silently, he backed away from the meadow. As soon as he could no longer see the cabin, he turned to go. He had taken only a few steps when he heard a shout.

"*¡Aquí! ¡Aquí!*" The voice came from a few yards away. Tucker saw the yellow robe crashing through the underbrush, heading straight for him. A third priest! He took off running, powered by fear and adrenaline. He lost the priest by circling around the crown of a hill and doubling back, but once again he could tell by their shouts that they had spread out. Tucker made a decision; he cut through a shallow ravine and climbed onto a piney ridge. It had to be here someplace—there!

The broken sword lay before the disko. In the faint light he could see the dried blood staining the pine needles. The wooden troll still stood guard exactly as Tucker had left it. The voices of the priests were getting louder. Tucker picked up the broken sword. Only a few inches of the blade remained attached to the haft. He cast it aside and edged closer to the surface of the disk. As before, it tugged at his shirt front.

He heard the snap of a stick breaking, very close. An instant later there came a flash; a bush a few feet away from him crackled and burst into flames.

Tucker threw himself into the disko.

# PART FIVE

# THE TOMB

The unreliability of the Timesweeps became evident almost immediately upon their conception. The Gnomon Chayhim accused the Boggsians of shabby work or, even worse, sabotage. The Boggsians, for their part, insisted that the devices had been built to specifications.

"If we build you a hammer and that hammer smashes your thumb, do not blame the hammer maker," said Netzah Whorsch-Boggs.

The Gnomon Chayhim pointed out several alarming and paradoxical time loops, such as the "Cat from Nowhere" that accompanied the Lah Sept Pure Girl on her journey from the Cydonian Pyramid to ancient Hopewell and back again. "The cat has no origin and no endpoint," said Chayhim. "This is unacceptable."

"The cat is of no consequence," declared Whorsch-Boggs.

"Tell that to the cat," said Chayhim.

—— $E^3$

## 30 FRANK-'N'-PORK

HENRY HALL, PERCHED ON A BARSTOOL AT THE PIGEON Drop Inn in downtown Hopewell, realized that he desperately needed to pee. He descended carefully from his stool — an operation rendered hazardous due to the large number of brandy manhattans he had consumed — and made his way unsteadily toward the restroom at the back of the bar.

The restroom door was locked. Henry banged on the door.

"Hold your horses!" the man inside shouted.

Henry stood swaying as he processed this information. The voice, he concluded, belonged to Big John Swenson. Henry knew Big John, a deliberate, slow-moving man who could turn a bowel movement into a half-hour project.

Henry did not think he could wait that long.

Dragging one hand against the wall to keep himself upright, he made his way to the back door and let himself out into the alley. He was surprised to find it dark outside. He had started drinking around lunchtime. He tried to add up how many drinks he had consumed, but his pickled brain refused to cough up an answer. Henry had never been much good at math.

He was leaning against the side of a Dumpster trying to remember what he was doing in the alley when the sudden slap of running feet on pavement caused him to look up. A bearded, helmeted, sandaled man wearing a short leather skirt and brandishing a stubby sword came racing down the alley. The man ran right past Henry, never slowing down, and disappeared around the side of the building.

Henry stared after him, blinking, feeling slightly miffed that the man had not stopped to chat. Must have been a hallucination. He'd had those before. Oh, well, another brandy manhattan would help sort it out. He had taken one lurching step toward the door when yet another impossibility came rolling, tumbling, or oozing into the alley.

Henry struggled to put a name to the thing he was seeing. All he could come up with was Frank-'n'-Pork, the 1,109-pound prize hog displayed at last year's Minnesota State Fair—but *this* Frank-'n'-Pork was legless, eyeless, and intensely, unrelentingly *pink*.

Henry, a third-generation hog farmer who had dealt with pigs of all types, stood his ground. Either this was some new breed of pig or, more likely, he was hallucinating again, in which case there was nothing to fear.

As it came closer, the Frank-'n'-Pork thing looked less like a hog and more like a large pink garbage bag filled with purposeful Jell-O. It flopped, wobbled, and gushed to a stop directly before Henry. Henry searched for a point of reference on the pulsing pink surface, but his eyes skittered here and there without finding purchase. After a few seconds, he noticed an aperture, no larger than a belly button, near what he took to be the thing's front end.

As Henry watched, the aperture expanded. By the time it reached the size of a basketball hoop, Henry could see a shimmering surface within, and he noticed his shirt front billowing out, as if the thing was attempting to inhale him.

The aperture quickly expanded into a pale, cloudy disk four feet in diameter. The creature—if it *was* a creature—was visible only as a fleshy pink band circling the edge of the disk.

By that time, Henry was too scared to care whether it was a hallucination or not. The disk was pulling at him, as if thousands of invisible fingers were tugging at every hair on his body. It wanted him.

*Run!* he thought—but his legs wouldn't move. He felt a trickle of warm pee running down his leg. He had just enough time to think, *Oh, yeah,* that's *what I came out here for,* when, with a popping, slurping, sucking sound, he was devoured.

The Timesweep remained perfectly motionless, its disko fully dilated. After several minutes had passed, the disko flickered green. With a sound like a rupturing water balloon, it vomited Henry Hall back into the alley.

Henry landed on his butt, his mouth wide open and his eyes bulging. The Timesweep contracted its portal and rolled, oozed, or tumbled off.

Carefully, Henry stood up. The last thing he remembered was sitting on a barstool enjoying a brandy manhattan. Now he was standing in the alley behind the Drop, wearing an unfamiliar one-piece garment that seemed to be made of gray polyester, and a pair of bright-blue plastic socks.

Henry had blacked out before, but he'd never woken up in somebody else's clothes. Even more curious, he had no hangover—no pounding headache, no sour taste in his throat, no roiling gut. In fact, he felt fantastic.

Weird. They would never believe him at the Drop. Of course, they never believed anything he said anyway, but at least they listened. He checked his garment, looking for pockets. There were none. No pockets meant no money. Oh, well, maybe he could parlay his story into a few free drinks.

Henry started for the back door to the bar, but before he reached it, he stopped, puzzled by something within himself. Something important was missing, as if he had forgotten to breathe. What was it? Henry's mind, working better than it had in many years, flipped through its catalog of wants, desires, and needs. Very shortly he had his answer: for the first time in more than twenty years, he had no desire whatsoever for a brandy manhattan—or any other alcoholic beverage.

Henry Hall pondered that for a few moments, shrugged, and began the long walk home.

# 31  THE HILL

Tucker landed on his feet and rolled, tumbling down a steep bank studded with broken stones and tufts of dry grasses. He came to rest against a prickly bush.

He blinked away the afterimages from the flash of the priest's weapon and looked up at the cloudless sky. The sun, already hot on his forehead, hung directly above.

He sat up, then stood. Except for a scrape on his elbow, he was uninjured. Looking around, he saw that he had rolled down the side of a dry ravine choked with thorny, small-leaved bushes. He could see the disko floating about ten feet above the lip of the ravine, winking in and out of sight as he moved his head from side to side. Would the priests come after him, or would they be afraid to enter the disko? He had no way of knowing. He watched the disko, ready to run if any yellow robes appeared.

After a few minutes, he decided that they weren't coming after him. Or maybe they had tried and ended up someplace else—Awn had told him that the diskos might take different people to different times and places. But what was *this* place?

She had also told him that the Klaatu used the diskos to witness "the terrible, the horrific, the irreversible." Did that mean something awful had happened here?

Using clumps of grass and stunted trees for handholds, Tucker climbed the steep side of the ravine. He slowed as he reached the lip, then peered cautiously over the edge and looked out over a rocky, dome-shaped hill. The hilltop was barren except for several irregularly spaced posts that looked like stubby, hand-hewn telephone poles with deep notches cut into their tops. The posts were about six feet tall, with one exception: at the center of the hill stood a taller post, almost twice as tall as the others.

The post closest to him was a few feet below and a few feet behind the disko. He could shinny up it, balance on the top, and dive into the disko if necessary. Of course, that might land him back in Awn's forest with the priests. Still, it was good to have an escape hatch.

Tucker climbed up over the lip of the ravine. Past the hilltop, a few hundred yards away, stood the stone walls of a city. He knew immediately that he was not in the twenty-first century — or anywhere near it. He could see no cars, no electrical wires, no highways. A faint haze hung low over the city walls — probably the source of the smoky smell hanging in the air. Between the hill and the city, several groups of people moved along a network of narrow dirt trails that fed into a wider road paved with stones. The road led to an open gate in the wall.

Some of the people carried baskets; others led donkeys doing the same. Most of them wore long dresses, or robes, in various colors. A man in a pale-blue sleeveless robe used a stick to guide a heavily laden camel along the base of the wall. A *camel*! Near the entrance to the city stood a group of men wearing helmets and red jerkins with armored breastplates. They carried swords on their belts. Tucker knew at once that they were soldiers.

This was not Minnesota, or even America. The people here probably didn't even speak English. He had no place to go, no food, no water . . . nothing. Had his father preceded him here? If so, he was not here now. Tucker wanted to curl into a ball and make it all go away. He closed his eyes and imagined himself back in Hopewell. Images flickered through his head: his mom at the organ, the swing at Hardy Lake, Lahlia, Kosh . . . Tucker drew a shaky breath. It all seemed so long ago.

*I'm older now,* he told himself. *Stronger.* This wasn't as bad as being on the World Trade Center or on that pyramid with the priests.

He opened his eyes. The hilltop was as before, but it felt somehow smaller. If his dad was here, Tucker would find him. If not, he would climb up that post, return to Awn's forest and try another portal.

The far side of the hill fell sharply into an orderly grove of trees with twisted trunks and silvery-green leaves—olive trees? Beyond the orchard lay a crazy quilt of bright green crops, and then sparse grassland giving way to brown desert. Tucker walked slowly around the crest of the hill—it was like standing on the dome of a giant, petrified skull that had pushed up through the earth's crust. Three brush-choked ravines radiated out from the crest. The one he had fallen into was the deepest and steepest of the three.

He looked at the walled city. If his father had arrived at this place, he would have had to seek food and shelter. He would have gone to the city. A narrow, shallow valley a few hundred yards across separated the city from the hill. Tucker did not like the look of the soldiers at the gate. A boy wearing gray coveralls and bright-blue plastic booties would definitely be noticed. He sat down with his back to one of the posts and considered his situation.

What would his father do? What had his father *done*?

The camel, the walled city, the way people were dressed all added up to his being somewhere in Africa or the Middle East. He wished he'd paid closer attention in his geography and history classes because, he thought with a sour smile, you never know when you might be magically transported halfway around the world and hundreds of years into the past. But the bigger question than *Where?* or *When?* was *Why?* Awn had said that the Klaatu Diskos led to *interesting times.* What made this place so interesting?

What had Awn said? *The death of a prophet.*

At the sound of leather scuffing stone, Tucker ran back to the ravine and hid behind a bush. Seconds later, a single soldier climbed onto the hilltop from the opposite side. He was dressed exactly like the man Tucker had seen running through Awn's forest.

The soldier lifted off his helmet, set it on the ground, wiped the sweat from his brow with his forearm, and ran his fingers through his short-cropped hair. He walked to the tall post, grabbed it with both hands, and shook it back and forth. The post wobbled. The soldier muttered something and trudged over into one of the other ravines. A few minutes later, he returned carrying an armful of flat rocks. He dumped the rocks next to the tall post, then fit one of the smaller rocks into a gap at the base of the post and used a larger stone to pound it into place. When he had finished, he stood and tried to shake the post again. This time, the post did not wiggle. Satisfied, the soldier repeated his task with two of the shorter posts. He retrieved his helmet, tucked it under his arm, and left the hilltop.

Tucker waited. Something would happen—it always did. Awn had told him that the diskos were inconstant but never random. There had to be a reason the portal had brought him to this place.

Two more soldiers, each of them carrying a long, forked pole, climbed onto the hilltop. They stopped near the tallest post and stood talking in low voices. Seconds later, they were followed by a squat, smiling man wearing a soiled brown tunic.

Around the man's tunic was a wide belt decorated with silver. In one hand he carried a mallet, in the other a leather sack. He joined the two soldiers, tossing the mallet and the sack on the ground near the base of the post. The sack made a clanking sound. The three men looked across the valley toward the walled city. The squat man made a joke; the soldiers laughed. Tucker raised himself higher to see what they were looking at.

Crossing the valley, headed in their direction, were three naked men carrying wooden beams across their shoulders. A group of about ten soldiers followed them closely. The soldiers could have been Greek, Egyptian, or any of a dozen other nationalities, but with a growing dread of what he was about to witness, Tucker felt certain they were Romans.

A crowd of perhaps thirty people wearing a variety of robes and tunics in various colors followed the Roman soldiers. Several children, dressed in tattered and stained fabric, ran in and out of the crowd, shouting and laughing. At the rear of the procession, several bearded men in long white robes walked two abreast.

One of the naked men at the front of the procession pitched forward. He fell flat, the weight of the beam driving his face into the dirt. Two of the soldiers grabbed the ends of the beam and lifted him to his feet. The man's arms were roped to the beam. He staggered forward, blood streaming from his nose.

Horrified, Tucker ducked back into the ravine. He did not think he could watch what was about to happen, even

though he'd seen it depicted in illustrations, in movies, and—
most vividly—in his imagination. He huddled there trying not
to listen as the voices—and the cries of pain—grew louder. He
pressed his hands to his ears and, for the first time since he had
left Hopewell, Tucker Feye prayed—for Jesus.

**32   IN THE TOMB**

The worst part — even worse than the screams and gasps and groans — was the sound of the mallet striking iron, again and again. The reality of what was happening on top of that hill could not possibly have been worse than what Tucker was seeing in his head: nails tearing through muscle, tendon, and bone. He forced himself to climb back up the side of the ravine. He peeked over the edge in time to see four of the soldiers using the forked poles, one on each end of the beam, to raise one of the men — the one who had fallen on his face — onto the tallest post. When the beam reached the top, it dropped with a thud into the notch, forming a T-shaped cross.

The man hanging from the cross appeared to be unconscious. The other two men had already been hung from two of the shorter posts.

The crowd watching the crucifixions were gathered at the far side of the hilltop. Tucker remembered the name of this hill:

Golgotha, the place of the skull. The man hanging from the tallest cross would be Jesus.

*The death of a prophet.*

The Roman soldiers formed a barrier, keeping the observers well back from the crosses. The white-robed men stood off to the side, separate from the rest. The cheerful man with the silver-studded belt brought his mallet over to the tall post and looked up at Jesus. The head of the mallet was stained with blood. The man, Tucker decided, must be the official crucifier, or executioner. He said something to one of the soldiers, who spat on the ground and turned away. Another soldier — the only one wearing a crest on his helmet — shouted an order. The soldier who had spat returned reluctantly to the base of the crucifix, removed his helmet, squatted down, and allowed the executioner to clamber onto his shoulders so that he could reach Jesus's feet. The executioner pulled a long, broad-headed nail from a pocket in his tunic. He used his palm to drive the point of the nail deep into Jesus's right ankle, then bent the leg and hammered the nail through the ankle into the side of the post. Blood spattered from the fresh wound, ran down his arm and dribbled onto the cursing soldier's head.

By this point, the scene had become so unreal that Tucker felt as if he were watching a particularly graphic and gruesome movie, but he could not look away. The executioner repeated his act with the other ankle. This time, as the executioner delivered the final blow with the mallet, the man on the cross shuddered and awakened with an agonized moan. The soldier, startled, staggered back and lost his balance. Both men fell backward, the executioner landing flat on his back.

The other soldiers laughed. The executioner and the soldier jumped to their feet, shouting at each other. Above them, on the cross, the dying man looked around with a wild-eyed expression of amazement and despair, as if he could not believe that he had come to this.

Tucker, cowering in the ravine, closed his eyes and began, silently, to weep.

The soldiers departed Golgotha — all but two, who squatted in the scant shadow cast by the dying prophet and played some sort of game involving polished stones and coins. The crowd of gawkers became bored and returned to the city. The men in the white robes were among the last to leave, but for a few of the unruly children, who stayed behind, laughing and calling out to the crucified men. Mired in their own miseries, the dying men ignored them. One of the children threw a handful of pebbles at Jesus. The pebbles bounced off the cross and rattled down upon the soldiers, who jumped up from their game and chased the children off.

Tucker waited in the ravine. Every few minutes, the man on the tallest cross would stir, moaning and muttering and trying to lift himself with his feet to take the pressure off his arms and chest, and then he would pass out again. The other two crucified men followed a similar pattern. Tucker had always thought of the crucifixion as equal parts holy and horrifying, but he could see nothing holy about any of this. The dying men were in agony. Jesus did not look at all like a man who believed he would be resurrected. He looked *scared.* And where was Mary, his mother? Where was Mary Magdalene? Where were the apostles and the rest of his followers?

One of the soldiers produced a wineskin. The two men passed it back and forth, drinking. Their conversation became loud and boisterous; one attempted to engage Jesus in conversation, but he was not satisfied by the dying man's anguished replies. The wineskin gave up its last drops; the soldiers grew sleepy. They arranged themselves with their heads in the shadow of the cross and soon were snoring.

*This might be a good time for me to leave,* Tucker thought. He could follow the ravine down to the base of the hill. From there, he could cut through the olive orchard and . . . after that, he wasn't sure. He would have to find food and shelter for the night—either that or go back through the disko to confront the priests.

A movement about fifty yards to his right caught his eye. A figure emerged from another ravine and crept across the stony expanse toward the tallest cross. It was his father, in jeans and a flannel shirt, wearing the bright-blue boots of the Medicants, exactly as he had been dressed the day he returned to Hopewell with Lahlia.

Tucker almost shouted but caught himself before the sound

left his throat. He did not want to awaken the two snoring soldiers. Instead, he stood and waved, but his father was focused on the man on the cross, and had his back to Tucker.

The Reverend Feye approached the cross. He looked up at Jesus and said something. Jesus groaned and stirred. The Reverend moved closer and spoke again, then reached up and touched the man's foot.

Jesus screamed, contorted his body, and passed out again.

The two soldiers sat up at the sound and looked around, confused. The Reverend Feye took off running, his long strides quickly taking him over the back side of the hill and into the olive orchard. Both soldiers started after him, but one of them stopped after a few strides, ran back to the tall cross, and thrust his sword deep into Jesus's side. Satisfied by the sudden and copious flow of blood, he joined his fellow soldier in pursuit of the Reverend Feye.

Tucker's first impulse was to go running after them, but he held back. Assuming his dad was able to elude the soldiers, where would he go? He would be interested in only one thing—the man who now hung slack and lifeless from that cross. Tucker thought there was a good chance he would return to the hilltop.

The soldiers had been gone for only a minute or two when another group appeared over the brow of the hill—the white-robed men who had earlier witnessed the crucifixion. Moving quickly and purposefully, they surrounded Jesus. One of them produced an iron tool from the sleeve of his robe and worked the nails loose from Jesus's ankles. Using the forked poles left behind by the soldiers, the others lowered him from the post—still attached to the crossbar. The man with the tool pulled the nails from his wrists. They wrapped him in a long white cloth and carried him off the hill in the opposite direction taken by Tucker's father and the two soldiers. Could his father have lured the soldiers away so that these men could steal Jesus's body?

The men carried the body off Golgotha using the path that led toward the city. Tucker followed them, staying out of sight. After a hundred yards or so, they turned away from the city onto a narrow road paved with irregular stones, where they were met by several other similarly garbed men. They followed the road along the valley, moving quickly, taking turns carrying their burden, looking back frequently. Tucker stayed off to the side, using rocks and the occasional shrub for concealment. His Medicant boots did an amazing job of protecting his feet from the plentiful sharp stones and thorns.

They walked for perhaps a mile, until they reached the base of a low cliff, a nearly vertical rock face about thirty feet high and several hundred yards long. Along its shadowed face were several rectangular openings. Some of the openings were blocked or partially blocked by stone slabs. Tucker watched from the opposite side of the road, hidden behind a cluster of bushes. The men set the body on the ground before one of the stone slabs. Using three round logs as crude wheels, they rolled the stone slab aside to reveal a low, narrow opening.

Two of the men carried the body inside. The others waited outside, pressing themselves close to the wall to take advantage of the scant midday shade.

By the time the men emerged from the cave, the sun had moved closer to the horizon. They rolled the slab back into place, then removed the rollers by twisting, rocking, and pulling at them until the bottom of the slab lay flat on the ground. The men talked for a few minutes, then headed back up the road toward the city.

*What will I see,* Tucker wondered, *if I sit here for three days?* Could that ruin of a man actually be Jesus Christ? Would he come back to life?

Tucker had always believed the story of Jesus in every detail, but after the blood and the horror he had seen, it seemed impossible that the crucified man could live again. And even if he were resurrected — assuming that it really *was* Jesus — what did that mean for Tucker? Would he join the men in white and become a boy apostle?

A flash of blue caught his eye. Farther down the road, the Reverend Feye stepped out from behind a pile of rocks and ran toward the sealed tomb. Tucker was about to shout out to him when nearby voices startled him to silence. Two men wearing faded red tunics were coming up the road, one of them carrying a dead goat over his shoulders. They were not the same men he had seen on Golgotha, but the hard-faced look of the professional soldier was unmistakable. Tucker ducked behind the bushes.

One of the soldiers noticed the oddly dressed man by the tomb and pointed him out to his companion. The Reverend was trying to pull the heavy stone away from the opening with his hands. The soldiers stopped and watched, first laughing at his efforts, then arguing with each other. Tucker understood none of the words, but he got the impression that they were trying to decide if it was worth their while to set aside their business with the dead goat long enough to arrest a possible grave robber. After a short discussion, the soldiers continued on down the road.

Tucker's father, intent on his work, had not noticed them. He tried to wedge one of the log rollers between the slab and the cliff. He couldn't get it in from the side, but after a minute he climbed on top and was able to force the end of the log between the rock face and the slab. Using the log as a pry bar, he pressed with his feet against the cliff and threw all his weight against the log. The slab teetered, then fell flat, breaking into two pieces. The Reverend landed on his feet, ducked his head, and entered the tomb.

**33   THE GOD CURE**

Tucker waited until the two soldiers with the goat were completely out of sight, then ran across the road and followed his father into the tomb. The passageway was only about five feet high and not much wider than his shoulders. To his relief, the tomb smelled only of moist stone, not of death.

"Dad!" he shouted. The soft rock absorbed the sound of his voice. He heard no reply. He moved deeper into the tomb and called out again. Still no answer. He waited a few more seconds for his eyes to adjust to the dark, then continued, feeling his way along the narrow passageway. After a few more yards it opened into a small chamber with just enough light for Tucker to make out the shapes of two stone boxes about three feet long by two feet wide. Another low opening led from the chamber deeper into the cliff. Tucker crouched and entered, feeling his way. He detected a silvery glow ahead. The passageway opened into another, larger chamber. Tucker stood up and stared at the source of the light: a Klaatu disko.

A surge of relief and hope caused Tucker to laugh out loud. The disko would take him back to Hopewell. After all, hadn't his father shown up there? All he had to do was take a few steps forward and he would be transported back home.

The room was empty except for two more of the stone boxes, and the swirling, glowing disk. He moved toward the disko, then hesitated. Where was Lahlia? The day his father had returned to Hopewell, he had brought Lahlia with him. But Tucker had seen him enter this tomb alone.

What did it matter? The important thing was to find his dad — and get home.

Another step, and he stopped again. Where was Jesus's body? Had it been fed into the disko? The thought came crashing in on him — maybe Jesus had been transported to the Medicants, who saved his life, then returned him to this tomb three days later. Tucker remembered the dead-looking man he had seen on the roof of the hospital. Had that been the same man he had seen crucified? And did that mean that this disk did *not* lead to Hopewell but rather to the roof of the Medicant hospital? And even if it did, he had no guarantee that he would end up in the same place as his dad. He might find himself with the priests again, or worse. Tucker took a step back and stared suspiciously at the disk's shimmering, treacherous surface.

"You are wise to be cautious."

Tucker spun around and started to fall backward toward the disko; the man who had spoken shot out a long arm and pulled him back. His father's gaunt face split into a smile. Tucker's heart lurched. "Dad?"

The Reverend Feye nodded. Tucker flung himself at his father and hugged him. The Reverend hugged him back — awkward as always, but warm and familiar — then held him out at arm's length. They studied each other in the lambent light of the disko.

"You have grown," said the Reverend.

"I—" The words caught in Tucker's throat. There was too much he had to ask, and on top of that was the shock of his father's appearance. This was not the Adrian Feye who had entered the tomb a few minutes earlier. This version of his father had dark, weathered skin, a grizzled, uneven beard, and gray hair hanging past his ears. He was wearing a dirt-stained white robe. Even more startling were the harsh lines etching his cheeks and the zealous gleam in his black eyes.

"You should not have come here," his father said.

A flash of anger loosened Tucker's tongue. "You *left* me!"

The Reverend's lips pressed together. He shook his head, then looked away and nodded slowly.

"You took *Mom*!"

The Reverend closed his eyes. "It was the only way," he said. "Her illness was incurable in our time. My only hope was that the Medicants could restore her." He looked to the disk, then at Tucker's blue-booted feet. "I see you have met them."

"They made me work in one of their factories for, like, two or three years. I don't even know how old I am!"

For several seconds, his father did not speak. "I'm sorry," he said at last. "Tell me how you got here."

"I went up on the roof and got sucked into the disko and landed on that pyramid."

"On the pyramid! You were there?"

"Yes." Tucker told him what had happened on the pyramid.

Tucker's father nodded. "I remember little of that. I arrived on the pyramid. The girl, Lahlia, was on the altar, and there were men in yellow robes. One of them touched me with a stick and . . . that's all I remember. I woke up in a Medicant hospital. They treated me and sent me on. I found myself in a strange forest filled with these . . . diskos, as you call them." He gestured at the disko.

"I was there too!" Tucker said. "Did you meet Awn? The old lady?"

"I saw an old woman there, but we did not speak."

"The priests from the pyramid came and killed her."

Tucker's father stared at him, his mouth working silently. "You saw this?" he said at last.

Tucker nodded. "They chased me. I saw the troll you carved, next to one of the diskos."

"The troll, yes . . . I found it on the roof of our house. I put it in my pocket. Later, I used it to mark the portal in the woods."

"I saw it. I followed you."

His father frowned. "I cannot believe all of this is random."

"Maybe it's God."

The Reverend shook his head dismissively.

Tucker felt himself getting mad. "You don't believe *anything*, do you?" Tucker said.

"I believe many things. I believe that this technology"—he gestured at the disko—"was created by human hands."

"What about Jesus? Wasn't that Jesus on the cross?"

"They call him Josua," said the Reverend. "And, yes, I believe that was him, but he is—he was—but a man."

"Is this why you came home that time and didn't believe in God anymore?"

"When I entered this tomb the first time, Josua's body was gone. I suspected that his resurrection, should it occur, would be engineered by the Medicants. But my loss of faith—it had nothing to do with any of this. Nothing I have seen here could have shaken my faith. More likely, it would have made it stronger. No, it was the Medicants who undid me. When I arrived in their hospital, I was not badly injured—not physically—but they cured me nonetheless."

"Cured you of what?"

"God."

"They cured you of *God*?"

"They cured me of irrationality. Of delusion. Of self-deception. Of faith." He coughed out a dry, humorless laugh. "I do not thank them for it, although I would not willingly return to my former state of ignorance."

Tucker stared at his father, who held his gaze for a moment, then looked away.

"The Medicants didn't make *me* not believe in God," Tucker said.

"Are you certain?"

Tucker considered, remembering the crucifixion he had witnessed and his mother playing the organ. He imagined God in heaven, a great, soothing light. He could feel His presence.

"God is real," he said. He was sure of it.

"Perhaps for you." His father shrugged. "But not for me."

"If you don't believe, why did you come back here?"

The Reverend smiled and slowly shook his head. "The first time I was here was by chance—or so I thought at the time. I was frantic and desperate. I saw much but I learned little. Does Josua return to life? His disciples sent him through this very disko, I am quite certain. Upon my first visit here, you must have seen me—the earlier me—enter this tomb, correct?"

Tucker nodded.

"I entered the disko, of course. It leads to a sort of dumping ground for Medicant failures, or at least it did when I passed through it. Josua's body was not waiting on the other side. The portals are inconstant."

"I thought it would go to Hopewell."

"Not directly. But eventually I found my way home. I will show you when we leave. When I came back to this place, I arrived at an earlier time. I've been waiting here for weeks."

"Waiting for what?"

"The resurrection. I've joined the Essenes—the men in

white who carried him here. I will be with them when, or if, Josua returns from the dead."

"What if Jesus *does* come back?"

"I will have questions for him."

Neither of them spoke for a few seconds, then Tucker asked the one question he had been afraid to ask.

"What about Mom?"

His father's shoulders sagged, and he lowered himself to sit on one of the stone boxes. Tucker felt his own heart pounding.

"Dad? Are you okay?"

"Sit down, Tuck."

With a feeling of dread swirling deep in his gut, Tucker sat beside his father and braced himself for whatever terrible news he was about to hear.

"I took your mother to see the Medicants. It was our last hope. They took her from me and"—his face crumpled—"she's gone."

"Gone? What do you mean, *gone*?"

His father shook his head slowly. "I mean gone."

"She's *someplace,* though, right?" Tucker said.

His father took a deep breath and said, "I'm sorry, Tuck. I don't know. They told me she had 'zeroed.' You know how they talk—all in numbers."

A cloud of numbness descended upon Tucker as he tried to understand. "She's dead?"

"What is dead?" His father gestured at the portal. "Are we alive now? I am no longer so certain." He lifted a burlap bag from his shoulder, set it on the dirt floor, and pulled out a bulging leather sack. He offered it to Tucker. "Drink. You must be thirsty."

Tucker took the water sack and drank. The water was warm and tasted of leather. He didn't care. His mom was dead, and he was sitting with his father in the tomb of Jesus, and nothing mattered. His father put a hand on his shoulder and gently squeezed. "I will take you home. Soon. Once my work here is complete. I—" The Reverend looked up sharply. "Did you hear something?" he whispered.

Tucker listened. He detected a faint sound.

The Reverend reached into his bag and pulled out a filthy, earth-colored robe. "Put this on. Quickly! It's probably just the Essenes returning. I can come up with a story to explain you, but do not let them see your feet or clothing."

Tucker pulled the robe over his head.

"It smells kind of goaty," he said.

"You'll get used to it."

A yellow flicker came from the passageway. A hand holding an oil lamp appeared, followed by a Roman legionnaire. Lamplight glittered off the soldier's polished breastplates. He let out a startled expletive when he saw the two robed figures standing in front of a glowing disk.

Tucker's father said something in a strange language. The soldier replied by barking a command. A second soldier emerged from the passageway. The Reverend smiled and spoke softly; the soldiers' voices were loud and guttural. Without warning, the first soldier stepped forward and struck Tucker's father on the side of the head with the pommel of his sword. The Reverend's knees buckled, and he went down. As the other soldier moved toward Tucker, the Reverend grabbed his ankle, tripping him.

"Go!" he shouted at Tucker.

Tucker shook his head. The Reverend scrambled to his feet and threw himself against the standing soldier, knocking him against the wall. The sword fell to the chamber floor. The Reverend snatched up the sword, but before he could do anything with it, the other soldier pulled a dagger from his belt and buried the blade deep in the Reverend's thigh. With a cry of pain, Tucker's father staggered back, keeping himself between the soldiers and Tucker. He grabbed Tucker's arm and pushed him back toward the disko. "Go! I'm right behind you." He gave Tucker a tremendous shove and sent him stumbling into the disko.

# 34  THE RECYCLING CENTER

Tucker landed on something soft, squishy, and lumpy. He had a moment to appreciate that, for once, he hadn't fallen on something hard and unforgiving, then he saw what had broken his fall: a dead man.

Tucker jumped up and backed away. The dead man was heavyset, with thinning gray hair, blue eyes, and pale skin. He was wearing a rumpled, old-fashioned-looking gray suit. Several dark holes ran in a line across his white dress shirt, from his right hip to his left shoulder, as if stitched with a machine gun.

Tearing his eyes away from the corpse, Tucker saw that he was in a round, domed room about fifty feet across. The floor was seamless metal. The walls, also metal, arched over his head to meet ten feet above him at a circular metallic armature surrounded by a complex tangle of cables and wires. At the center of the armature was a shimmering gray disk.

Tucker and the dead man were the room's only occupants. He moved as far from the corpse as he could get, sat with his back against the curved wall, and waited. The metal felt warm like skin, but hard and smooth. He counted the seconds, but his father did not appear. Either the Romans had killed him or the disko had taken him to some other place.

Minutes ticked by, the only sound a faint hum from the disko above. What had his father called this place? *A dumping ground for Medicant failures.*

Although the corpse was the last thing he wanted to see, it was hard not to look at it. He tried to imagine it as a peculiar rock formation but could only maintain the illusion for a few seconds at a time before he again saw it for what it was: a dead man. He had been sitting there for what felt like an hour when he noticed that the corpse appeared to be sinking slowly into the floor.

*Good,* he thought. Better to be alone than with that thing for company. But his curiosity soon drove him to take a closer look at how the body could be sinking into a solid metal floor. He got down on his hands and knees and peered closely at the point where the body met the floor. It took him a moment to understand what he was seeing, and when he did, he still didn't believe it.

The corpse wasn't sinking; it was being devoured by an army of ants. Except they weren't ants. They were tiny ant-size machines, and they were coming out of the floor. More precisely, they seemed to be *growing* from the floor. Tucker watched, too fascinated to be grossed out, as the machines formed themselves from the metal of the floor, beginning as tiny blobs like beads of sweat, then becoming more complex until, after about five seconds, they would detach themselves from the floor, crawl on miniature treads to the corpse, and, using tiny bladelike scoops, cut off a piece of clothing, or skin, or fat—never larger than the head of a pin—then melt back into the floor, carrying their prize with them. At any given moment, several thousand of the tiny machines were tearing the body apart bit by bit.

Tucker leaned down and blew on one of the miniature robots, flipping it onto its side. The machine's treads continued to roll, causing it to spin in futile circles. After a few seconds it stopped moving and melted back into the floor.

Tucker felt something moving between the floor and his knee. He jumped to his feet with a shout, brushed frantically at his robe, and stomped his feet up and down. A sprinkling of minirobots fell to the floor. He ran back to his place by the wall, breathing hard, and stared at the floor beneath him, ready to stamp out any reinforcements.

His father had been here, and he had survived. That meant there had to be a way out. Other than in a million pieces.

More machines pimpled the floor around his feet. When Tucker moved to the side, the pimples sank back into the base metal. As long as he moved every minute or so, the minirobots ignored him, but if he stood still, a new crop would form around his feet.

The dead man continued to lose mass—about a third of

him had been devoured. Had something like this happened to his mom? Had she died in a Medicant hospital to be eaten by tiny machines? The image was intolerable. Tucker pushed back the thought and walked slowly around the perimeter of the room, running his hand along the wall, feeling for a concealed doorway. He could not find even a hint of a seam in the warm metal surface.

By the time he had circled the room a dozen times, the corpse had completely disappeared and the machines were following Tucker en masse. He could no longer avoid them by moving every few moments. Each step he took produced an immediate response; the tiny bumps in the floor came and went within seconds. He figured he could keep moving for a few hours, but he couldn't walk in circles forever. Did the machines care that he was alive? Did they know?

He stopped and watched the machines form around his feet. Squatting, he pressed his palm to the floor. Several of the tiny robots trundled over. He forced himself to leave his hand there long enough for the robots to nip into his flesh. It felt like being poked by a dozen pins at once. Tucker jerked his hand up, stomped the rest of the robots off his feet, and continued to walk. Maybe by sampling his flesh, the robots would realize that he was alive.

Moments later, his offering of flesh seemed to have an effect, but not the one he had hoped for. The entire surface of the floor changed texture, becoming sandpaper-rough as thousands of machines formed on the surface. Each of them emitted a tiny puff of smoke. The hazy, vaporous layer rose up from the floor, becoming fainter as it climbed up his robe. By the time the haze reached his chest he could feel himself growing dizzy. Moments later his knees buckled and, with his last glimmer of consciousness, he sank to the floor.

# 35 EXIT TECH SEVERS 294

Tucker opened his eyes. He recognized the ceiling, or rather its color: the most neutral beige imaginable. He was lying on his back on what felt like a thin mattress. A low mutter came from his right; he turned his head. A bug-eyed alien wearing gray coveralls stood a few feet away. It reached out a gloved hand and touched his abdomen. Tucker felt a prickle of fear, but the fear faded as quickly as it had come, driven off by a soothing, numbing wave of comfort radiating out from his belly.

"Point four cc tramophine," said the creature.

Tucker realized that he was looking at a human being—a woman, by the sound of her voice—wearing cups of metallic mesh over her eyes. Her silver hair was cropped close to her scalp, and several black, jewel-tipped wires sprouted from her ears like antennae.

"Anxiety levels falling. One point two," she said. Her accent was weird, but he could understand her. He could see her eyes through the mesh. She was not looking at him; her eyes were focused on something he could not see. Tiny lights flickered across her irises. He felt weirdly peaceful and calm.

"Level zero point five," the woman said.

"Where am I?" Tucker asked.

"Mayo One Fourteen."

He wasn't sure if that was an answer to his question — she still wasn't looking at him.

"Are you a Medicant?"

She did not answer his question.

"What's your name?" he asked.

"Exit Tech Severs two nine four."

"That's your *name*?"

She turned to face Tucker. "Yes."

"Are you going to make me into a work zombie?" he asked.

Exit Tech Severs frowned slightly and returned her attention to the lights dancing on her eyes. "Injuries level one. Minor contusions, dehydration, anxiety level zero point four seven."

Tucker sat up. He was wearing only a pair of filmy shorts and the same blue foot coverings, but this time there was no tube affixed to his abdomen. A man with antennae sprouting from his ears, but no eye cups, was standing beside the open doorway. In his right hand was a device about the size of a cell phone, which he held pointed at Tucker.

"Can I have my clothes?"

Exit Tech Severs was speaking rapidly, but not to Tucker, or to the guard. "Internal functions normal, mentation twentieth-century neurotypical, immune system ninety-nine point seven percent operative; patient appears alert . . ." She cocked her head and appeared to be listening to something. After a moment, she turned toward Tucker and said, "Certain of your functions have been enhanced."

"Are you talking to me?" he asked.

"We have harvested your appendix."

"You took out my appendix?"

"We harvested its contents. The appendix is a rich source for atavistic bacteria. You should suffer no noticeable effects. Is this acceptable?"

"What if it's not?"

"The bacteria will be reintroduced to your abdominal cavity."

"Oh. No, thanks. How come you're even talking to me? Last time I was here, nobody told me anything."

Exit Tech Severs was staring into space again, absorbing information from her eye cups. "You have been here before," she said after a few seconds.

"I was in a place just like this. Only the people had colored buttons on their chests and these metal things on their heads. With lights on them."

"That technology is obsolete."

"Are you a Klaatu?"

"Klaatu are discorporeal."

"You mean they're ghosts," Tucker said.

Exit Tech Severs hesitated before replying. "Yes."

"What was that place I was in? With the dead guy."

"The portal that delivered you here is one of several our techs have captured and adapted."

"What do you mean, 'adapted'?"

"The portals have been acquired from various locations and moved here." She opened a compartment under his bed and handed him his coveralls and the robe his father had given him. "Clothe yourself and come with me."

Tucker pulled on the coveralls but left the robe behind. He followed Exit Tech Severs out of the room into the hallway. The guard stayed close behind.

"Where are we going?" he asked.

"You are being discharged," she said.

The floor shuddered. An instant later came a sound like muted thunder. The guard went rigid.

"What was that?" Tucker asked.

Exit Tech Severs's lips were moving, but she was making no sound.

"Was that thunder?" Tucker asked.

"No. Come with me." They followed the hallway to an elevator and ascended. As before, the elevator opened onto a rooftop. It looked like the same roof they had taken him to the first time, but instead of one disko, there were five of them, trapped within a framework of metallic girders and cables.

Beyond the rooftop, the city spread in all directions, as far as he could see. A plume of smoke was rising from a nearby structure. Tucker started toward the edge of the roof to get a better look, but the guard grabbed him by the arm.

An explosive sound hammered Tucker's ears; the building shifted violently. Exit Tech Severs lurched against him and the guard, and the three of them fell to their knees. One of Exit Tech Severs's eye cups popped off and skittered across the roof-top. Her eye was blue. An instant later they heard several more explosions. The hum from the captured diskos seemed to get louder.

"What's going on?" Tucker asked.

Exit Tech Severs consulted her remaining eye cup. "This unit is under attack."

"By who?"

"Lambs," said Exit Tech Severs.

"Plague," muttered the guard.

"What plague?"

"There is no plague," said Exit Tech Severs. "The Lambs' religious frenzy precludes all rational thought. You must go now."

The guard hoisted Tucker to his feet and pushed him toward the leftmost disko.

"Where does it go?" Tucker asked Exit Tech Severs.

"I do not have that information."

"What information do you have?"

"Portal two three seven emanates particles in accord with

certain aspects of your genetics. You are being returned to your proximate point of origin."

Tucker considered the previous places he had been. The chances that he would end up someplace he didn't want to revisit were daunting. "What if I refuse to go?"

Exit Tech Severs fixed him with her cupless eye and tipped her head toward the guard. "The facilitator will enforce your departure."

Another explosion shook the building.

Tucker took a deep breath and stepped into the disko.

# PART SIX

# HOPEWELL

*Iyl Rayn, seeing her carefully placed diskos being captured, modified, and sometimes consumed, decided to take action.*

*Cloned avatars were not unknown to the Klaatu—they had long been used to facilitate communication with corporeals and to perform other tasks requiring the manipulation of matter. Although actual memories could not be projected into a clone, it was a simple matter for the Boggsians to create a blank using DNA obtained from each individual Klaatu prior to his or her discorporation. This blank clone would be grown to adulthood in a virtual-reality crèche, where it would be imbued with such attitudes, beliefs, ethics, and information deemed suitable by its Klaatu originator. Multiple avatars were possible, though the practice was frowned upon by the Cluster.*

*Iyl Rayn, undeterred by the objections of her peers, ordered a trio of cloned bodies from the same Boggsian technicians who had constructed her diskos. She then set about designing an education for each of her avatars, with special attention given to those qualities she felt she had lacked during her own flesh-and-blood existence.*

— **E**³

## 36   YAR LIA

Kosh Feye popped open another can of beer, walked unsteadily out of his workshop, swung one leg over the seat of his Harley, made himself comfortable, and took a sip.

*Probably not a good idea to go for a ride,* he told himself. Nine beers was nine too many.

He took a bleary look around at his little slice of heaven.

Garden needed weeding.

Barn door half off its hinges.

Adrian's Chevy parked all kittywampus, with the windows open.

No Tucker.

Kosh took another swig of beer. He couldn't believe that he missed having that kid around. He thought about Adrian. His brother had asked him to do one thing in fifteen years—take care of the kid for a few weeks—and Kosh had failed. He thought about the day Tucker had wrecked the dirt bike. He'd been furious, but at the same time, he'd been seeing himself at that age, just as boneheaded and suicidal. No, not suicidal, just not thinking that he could ever die. And now Tucker was gone, maybe dead.

His thoughts returned to Hopewell. The girl, Lahlia, jumping into that thing on the roof. He had no doubt that Tucker had preceded her. What had they been thinking? He should have gone after them. He had tried. He really had. But he had hesitated too long. The disk had disappeared.

Kosh had stayed in Hopewell for two weeks, waiting. The Beckers, of course, searched everywhere for Lahlia. Kosh endured several interrogations from the Hopewell County Sheriff. He did not tell the police that he had seen the girl disappear into a magic disk—that would have landed him in another institution. Ronnie Becker also fell under suspicion, but with no evidence against either of them, the police turned their attention to searching the fields and woods with an army of volunteers, and investigating rumors of suspicious strangers.

They found nothing. The girl—and Tucker—had simply disappeared.

The disk never returned. After another week, Kosh closed up the house and drove home to Wisconsin. And began to drink.

It wasn't helping.

Kosh leaned back on his bike and looked up at the roof of the barn. He squeezed his eyes closed, then looked again.

"Son-of-a . . ." It was back. He fell off the bike but managed not to spill his beer.

One minute later he was dragging his extension ladder over to the barn. The ladder was tall enough to bypass the missing rungs. Kosh climbed, still holding his beer, and soon found himself standing shakily on top of the roof, glaring at the pulsing disk.

He let out a string of curses. The disk absorbed his words without comment. He took another gulp of beer and wiped his mouth with his leather sleeve. Part of him wanted to jump into the disk—if only to punish himself for not going after Tucker and the girl when he'd had the chance. But what then? Would he arrive on top of the World Trade Center again? He could bring his own ladder. He might find Tucker there. He might be able to bring him back. . . .

A tendril of black smoke snaked out from the disk. Kosh inhaled through his nose. The unmistakable tang of burning jet fuel. Fire and brimstone. Were the towers already in flames? If so, the disk might deliver him to a time *after* the towers collapsed. He would fall a thousand feet onto a pile of smoking rubble. And even if he did find Tucker again, would it be the same Tucker? Did the disk in Hopewell also lead to the Twin Towers?

The disk's surface swirled into a pattern he had not seen before, a sort of stuttering, grainy spiral, then flashed bright green. A small, slim figure leaped from the disk and landed lightly upon the roof.

It was a girl, maybe seventeen or eighteen years old, with long yellow hair tied back and dark eyes hard as stone. She wore a sleeveless black tunic with a metallic sheen to it, black leggings, and thick-soled black boots.

"Hello, Kosh," she said, looking from his unshaven face to the can of beer dangling from his fingers.

"Do I know you?" said Kosh.

"You don't remember me?" She half smiled.

Kosh squinted, trying to bring her into better focus. A fine white scar, beginning at the corner of her left eye, scrolled down her cheek to her jaw. It actually looked good on her.

He said, "Lahlia?"

"I am Lah Lia no longer. I am the Yar Lia. You can call me Lia."

"You're old. I mean, older 'n you was."

She regarded him with a look of disappointment.

"You're drunk," she said.

Kosh nodded; there was no point in denying it.

"How long will it take for you to get sober?"

Kosh took the question literally. "Four or five hours," he said. "Depending how sober you want me. Not that I see much point in it." He gestured with his beer to include both the girl and the disk. "This all makes way more sense when I'm wasted."

She took the can of beer from him, sniffed it, made a face, and dropped it.

"Hey!" Kosh said.

The can rolled down the roof, leaving behind a trail of foam, and disappeared over the edge. Kosh heard a faint clank as the can landed on something metallic—probably his bike.

"Tucker is in trouble," she said.

"Tucker?" A surge of hope cut through his alcoholic haze. "He's okay?"

"No. He needs us."

"Us?"

"Yes. Do you think you can climb down off this roof without killing yourself?"

"I have no idea," Kosh said honestly.

She rolled her eyes. "Come on." She held out her hand. "Let's get you sobered up."

Kosh began to tilt to the left. She grabbed his arm to steady him. He tried to pull his arm free, but the girl's grip was uncommonly strong. Kosh looked over her head at the disk, and the old fear came crashing back.

"Do I have to go in that thing again?"

"We do not need a Gate to get where we're going," said the Yar Lia. "We can take your bike."

**37 PIGEON DAZE**

Tucker landed on his feet. *I'm getting good at this,* he thought, looking around. He was on yet another roof. The disko floated several feet above his head. The roof was flat, large, covered with tiny gray pebbles pressed into soft asphalt, and surrounded by a knee-high wall. Tucker approached the wall and looked down onto a street four stories below. He knew at once that he was looking at the busy main street of a small town. Cars were angle-parked, facing into the crowded sidewalks. There was some sort of festival happening. Several vendor carts along the sidewalks were selling minidonuts, hot dogs, and other carnival foods. Except for the cars and people and all the vendors, it looked a lot like Hopewell. In fact—was that Krause Hardware across the street? And, two doors down, the Pigeon Drop Inn.

*Hopewell!*

Tucker's chest swelled, and tears filled his eyes. He knew exactly where he was—on the roof of Hopewell House, the old, boarded-up hotel. No sign of murderous priests, scary pyramids, or frozen-faced Medicants. This was *his* Hopewell. He looked back at the disko that had delivered him. Was it the same disko that had delivered Lahlia to Hopewell? How many diskos *were* there in Hopewell?

Tucker tried to pick out a familiar face, but the crowd below was made up of strangers who didn't have that small-town look. Some were too well dressed, like the portly man wearing a suit and eating a hot dog, and the woman next to him in high heels and a white dress. Others looked like tourists, in jeans, colorful shirts, clean athletic shoes, and sunglasses. Many had binoculars or cameras hanging around their necks. A lot of the people looked Hispanic. That wasn't unusual—a lot of seasonal workers showed up in Hopewell for the harvest. Several young people wearing yellow T-shirts were moving about in small groups.

He spotted old Emil Janky outside his barbershop, shooing away a cluster of yellow-shirted teens who were blocking his doorway. That was reassuring—for a few seconds, he had feared the entire population of Hopewell had been replaced by strangers. Leaning out over the parapet, Tucker looked toward his father's church, but his view was obstructed by a large banner strung across Main Street:

# HOPEWELL PIGEON DAZE
## September 27 – 29

*Pigeon Daze?* Tucker could make no sense of that—unless he'd gone back to when Lorna Gingrass had killed those two passenger pigeons. . . . But no, the cars were all later models. This had to be about the same time he had left. Except, according to the banner, it was now September.

He found a large trapdoor on the southeast corner of the roof, pulled it open, climbed down a steel staircase, pushed through another doorway to enter the hotel's fourth floor, and stared in astonishment.

The last time he had been in Hopewell House—he and the Krause brothers had sneaked in one day—it had been home only to barn swallows, paper wasps, bats, and dust. What he saw now was a pristine hallway with fresh paint and new carpeting, illuminated by a row of ornate wall sconces. An enormous mirror hung at the end of the hallway. Tucker approached it slowly, gawking at his new self: a lanky young man with a soft, patchy beard, a longer chin than he remembered, and floppy hair hanging nearly to his shoulders. His gray coveralls made him look like a janitor, or an escaped prisoner—except for the blue plastic boots. Moments earlier he had been eager to run out onto the street and find a familiar face, but now he wondered if anybody would recognize him. And even if they did, there would be questions. He was not ready for questions. He needed time to think. And new clothes. A barrage of problems tumbled through his head: he had no money, he didn't even live in Hopewell anymore, he still had no idea where his mother had gone, and his father . . . Was his dad even alive? The only way to find out would be to somehow return to the tomb.

He turned his back on the mirror and forced himself to make a mental list. Clothes. Food. Then what? Call Kosh? No, first he would check to see if his mom or dad had made it home. He could find some normal clothes there, and there might still be some canned or dried food in the pantry. After that, he could figure out his next step.

It wasn't much of a plan, but it would have to do.

With so many people on the streets, nobody paid attention to Tucker as he made his way down the sidewalk. Several new shops had opened. Every store displayed pigeon products: pigeon mugs, pigeon postcards, pigeon T-shirts, and other souvenir items. The pigeons depicted were not normal pigeons but passenger pigeons. The new pizzeria was advertising something called a Passenger Pigeon Pie. He hoped it wasn't made of real passenger pigeons.

Yellow T-shirts were everywhere, all with the same imprint: HE IS COMING! on the front and THE LAMBS OF SEPTEMBER on the back. Most of them were worn by teens.

He was walking behind a trio of yellow-shirted teenage girls when one of them—a girl with long blond hair—looked back and gave him a big smile.

"Are you coming tonight?"

"Coming where?"

The girls stopped walking and turned to him.

"To the *revival*!" the blond girl said, as if she could not believe he didn't know about it.

"I don't think so," he said.

"You should," she said, suddenly all serious. "He could come tonight."

"Who?"

"Jesus!"

Tucker thought about the dead man hanging from the cross.

"All the signs are here," said the girl. "The miracles and everything. And the birds."

"What birds?"

"The *passenger* pigeons," said all three of them at once, giving him exactly the same look—a look that said he was clearly insane.

Another of the girls, the smallest and prettiest of the three, looked closely at Tucker. "Did you used to go to school here?"

"No," Tucker said, even as he recognized her. Kathy Aamodt. She was in the same grade as him at school—Tom Krause's crush.

She looked at him even more closely. "You kind of look like this guy that used to go to our school," she said. "But you're older."

Tucker figured it was best to change the subject. "What's the deal with the pigeons?" he asked.

"Are you, like, from another planet?" asked the blond girl.

"I'm from Bulgaria," Tucker said.

"The passenger pigeons came back. Thousands of them. It's been all over TV and everything."

"I haven't been watching the news."

"A whole flock was roosting in a tree by Hardy Lake last week, and they were all up by Grouse Creek this morning. People get on buses and follow them. Nobody knows where they came from."

"The birds or the people?"

"The *birds*! God sent them as a harbinger."

Tucker had his own ideas about how the passenger pigeons had come to Hopewell.

"You should definitely come see Father September tonight," the blond girl said.

Tucker remembered Lahlia talking about a new preacher taking over the Church of the Holy Word. The so-called miracle worker. A creepy feeling ran up his spine. There had been a time when he might have believed in a preacher who performed miracles, but after all he had seen recently, he suspected that this "Father September"—and the passenger pigeons—had more to do with diskos than with miracles.

The girls told him that the revival was in the county park, just south of town. Tucker promised to be there, then continued walking up Main Street. Hopewell was small enough that he quickly left downtown behind. He was halfway home when someone on a bicycle appeared ahead, riding toward him. Tucker recognized Will Krause. Will pulled up in front of Tucker and stared at him, openmouthed.

*"Tucker?"*

Tucker nodded.

"You got a beard! You're taller, too!"

"I had a growth spurt."

"No kidding. Jeez. You look like—like you're old enough to vote! What happened to you? Tom said you must have run off with Lahlia."

"Lahlia is gone?"

"She disappeared the same time you did. The Beckers think she got kidnapped. Some people think she ran off with you. I figure she took off to get away from Ronnie since he's kind of a dick."

"Ronnie's still around?" Tucker had the same feeling about Ronnie Becker.

"Yeah, he's all religious now, but he's still a dick."

"What about this preacher who does miracles?"

Will rolled his eyes. "Supposed miracles. Like making blind people see and stuff. He predicted the pigeons would return, and then they did, and then he predicted all this other stuff. My dad says it's all hooey. He says September's a phony, and his so-called miracles are all fake. Like, he made this blind lady see, but there's no way to know if she was really blind to start out with. And the pigeons might have already been here. The only good thing is that he's against math. They say you shouldn't teach math or algebra in school. That would be cool. No algebra."

Tucker thought about Awn and her aversion to numbers.

Will looked down at Tucker's feet. "What kind of shoes are those?"

"Oh, just something I got in Wisconsin. How's Tom doing?" he asked.

Will's face clouded. "I don't really know. He hasn't been around much. I was hoping I might see him in town. He joined up with the Lambs. He's what they call a Pure Boy. Some sort of altar boy, I guess. My dad was, like, 'You're going straight to hell, young man!' Mom's totally freaked."

"You're kidding me. *Tom?*" The Tom Krause he knew was no more religious than a cat.

"I think he's just doing it because Kathy Aamodt joined up," Will said.

That made more sense.

"Where you going?" Will asked.

"Home."

"Like, to your house?" Will gave him an odd look.

"Yeah. Why?"

"Um . . . I think there's somebody else living there now."

**38 A TIME TO PRAY**

A BLACK SUV WAS PARKED IN FRONT OF THE GARAGE, and someone had mowed the lawn. Tucker stopped at the end of the driveway and stared up at the roof. The disko wasn't there. He walked to the front door and raised his hand to knock, then thought, *Why knock?* It was his house.

He opened the door and walked in. The furniture in the living room was the same, but the house smelled different. The coffee table was piled with unfamiliar books and magazines. Everything seemed smaller.

He heard the sound of running water and went to the kitchen. A woman with long red hair was standing at the sink, wearing one of his mother's dresses.

"Hello?" he said. His voice sounded hollow and distant.

The woman turned, let out a startled yelp, and dropped the pan she was holding.

Tucker's heart stopped. The pan clattered on the floor.

It was his mother. Except it wasn't. This Emily Feye looked like his mom in his parents' wedding photos—a young woman of twenty.

"Mom?" he heard himself say.

She yelled something—it sounded like *Tamm!*—and edged toward the back door.

Tucker said, "Wait!"

The screen door banged open and a man with curly black hair and a yellow T-shirt rushed into the kitchen. He fixed his eyes on Tucker, ran at him, and threw a punch. Tucker easily avoided the fist, grabbed the man's arm, and swung him against the stove.

Even as it was happening, Tucker thought, *When did I get so fast?*

A ceramic pitcher exploded against the cupboard.

Tucker ducked and shouted, "Mom! Cut it out! It's me!"

The younger Emily Feye did not stop. She flung a plate at him, then a coffee cup—anything she could grab off the counter. The plate struck him on the shoulder, the cup shattered against the wall, and the man came at him again from behind and wrapped an arm around Tucker's throat. Tucker threw himself forward, flipping the man over his shoulders and slamming him to the floor.

The woman reached for another plate.

"Stop it!" Tucker shouted. "This is my house!"

The woman hesitated, looking from Tucker to the man on the floor.

"I *live* here!" Tucker said.

The man groaned and pushed himself up.

"Who are you?" the woman asked. It was his mother's voice, but with an odd accent.

"Who are *you*?" Tucker countered.

The man regained his feet and started toward Tucker again.

"Tamm, wait," said the woman.

The man stopped.

"He says this was his house," she said.

"It is *our* house," said Tamm. His accent was stronger than hers.

Tucker ignored him and stared fiercely at his mother — or the younger version of his mom — trying to make sense of it. Was this his mom before she had given birth to him? Before she had married his dad? She looked just as bewildered as he felt.

"I live here," he said.

"*We* live here," said Tamm. "We have permission." He pronounced it *pair-miss-own*.

"Permission from who?"

"Father September. You go now."

The woman said, "Tamm . . ."

"He must go," said Tamm. He turned to Tucker with his fists clenched. "You go *now*."

"Okay, okay," Tucker said, "but this is still my house."

The woman set the plate back on the counter. "You say you lived here?" she asked in the soft, sane voice that Tucker had not heard since before his mother had gotten sick. Was it possible that she hadn't died, that the Medicants had cured her—and made her young again? But then where did she get that accent?

"I lived here. My whole life. And so did you. Don't you remember anything?"

She shook her head, confused.

"You don't recognize me?" Tucker said.

She stared hard at him, then shook her head again.

"I'm your *son*!" It came out like a sob; he felt as if his chest was crumbling from the inside out.

"I have no son," said the woman.

Tucker stared at her. He could hear himself breathing. He could hear his heart beating in his ears. "How did you get so young?" he asked in a ragged whisper. "You can't be more than nineteen or twenty."

She winced as if he had slapped her.

"You were twenty when I was born," Tucker said.

Tamm made an animal sound deep in his throat and again advanced upon Tucker. He seemed to be moving in slow motion. Tucker stepped easily aside and gave Tamm a shove, using Tamm's own momentum to send him headfirst through the screen door.

"Tamm!" the woman screamed and ran to him. Tamm moaned and, with her help, slowly extracted himself from the torn screen.

"I'm sorry," Tucker said.

She looked over her shoulder at Tucker and said, "You have done enough. Look, he is bleeding!"

Blood trickled from a small cut on Tamm's forehead.

"Go and talk to Father September," she said. "If he wants us to leave this place, we will go. Until then, this is our home."

"Where do I find him?"

"At the church," she said.

"You really don't know me?" he asked.

"I have never seen you before."


On the walk back to town, Tucker tried to figure out what had just happened. His dad, back in the tomb, had told Tucker she was "gone," that the Medicants had told him she "zeroed." Maybe "zeroed" didn't mean she was dead, but that they had erased her memories and made her young again. But then how had she ended up with that guy Tamm?

The other weird thing was how easily he'd been able to fight off the older, bigger man. When Tamm had attacked him, his perceptions had sped up, and he had suddenly felt stronger and quicker. Tucker picked up a jagged stone the size of an egg, drew his arm back, and threw it. The rock sailed out over Aamodt's cornfield and landed somewhere on the other side, well over two hundred yards away.

That wasn't normal.

*We have enhanced certain of your functions,* the Medicant woman had told him.

What had they done to him? He tried jumping straight up. He got a little higher than he expected, but nothing any basketball player couldn't do. Too bad — for a second there, he'd hoped he could fly. But being strong and fast was good.

He continued toward town, walking more quickly. He imagined himself going back to the tomb in Jerusalem, fighting off those Roman soldiers, saving his dad, telling him that Mom was alive. If the disko on his house reappeared, he could go to the pyramid, then jump through the disko that led to Awn's woods, and from there he could get to Golgotha . . .

He thought about his mother again, and the fantasy of saving his father fell away. It didn't help that he was stronger and faster. His mother was alive, but he had lost her just the same. He slowed as a feeling of utter isolation overwhelmed him — he wanted to collapse there by the side of the road and be absorbed into the earth. Tucker stopped and closed his eyes. *Nothing,* he thought, *is worse than being alone.* And then it hit him that he was not alone.

There was God. A wave of guilt swept away his other emotions. The last time he had actually *prayed* had been on Golgotha.

Had the Medicants taken away his faith, as they had his father's?

He tried to imagine God looking down on him. For a moment he felt a terrible blankness, a sense of being anchorless and forsaken. A panicky feeling rose up inside him. He opened his eyes and looked at the gently sloping field of corn to his left, at the cattail marsh to his right. Straight ahead, he could see the top of Hopewell House poking above the horizon. If God was not making his presence known at the moment, then so be it. Maybe God was with this Father September, who had supposedly given away his home and who also — if what Will and the girls in town said was true — was able to predict the future.

Maybe this was a test of his faith. He could pray later.

First, he had business with this new preacher.

# 39  THE ORGAN MECHANIC

THE FRONT OF THE SMALL CHURCH WAS MUCH AS TUCKER remembered. Even the sign — THE HOLY WORD — was unchanged. Four teenage girls selling T-shirts were blocking the front steps. Tucker walked up to the one who seemed to be in charge, a tall girl with curly brown hair and glasses.

"Is Father September in there? I need to see him," he said.

The girl laughed; her friends provided an echo of giggles.

"*Everybody* wants to talk to him," she said, looking him up and down. "Only you don't look like a reporter. Anyways, he doesn't see anybody."

Tucker ignored her and started up the steps to the double doors. The girls moved aside and watched him. Tucker tugged on the doors. Locked. The doors had never been locked before; his father had always been proud of that fact. *What would they steal?* he had once said. *Salvation? Forgiveness? Truth?*

The doors opened suddenly, almost knocking Tucker off the steps. A thin young man with a shaved head, a wiry dark beard, and deep-set dark-brown eyes looked out at him.

"I am sorry. No admittance." He had the same peculiar accent as the man at the house. And he didn't look sorry at all.

"Are you Father September?" Tucker asked.

The man tried to close the door. Tucker wedged his foot against it, holding it open.

"I need to see Father September."

"You cannot—" He broke off, looking down at Tucker's blue-clad foot. "Ah," he said. "A fellow traveler. Enter, friend. I am Brother Koan."

Tucker's heart began to race. His Medicant boots were his ticket to see Father September, which confirmed his suspicions. The miracle-working preacher had traveled the diskos.

Inside, the church was exactly as he remembered: twenty rows of pews, the modest limestone altar, and standing proudly behind it, the great organ, its cluster of pipes reaching toward heaven.

Brother Koan pointed toward the back of the church. "You will find him there."

Behind the wall of organ pipes was a small sacristy. Tucker looked inside. The room was empty except for a narrow cot, a sink, a wooden chair, and a small desk. He heard faint muttering coming from beneath the organ. A pair of bare legs and sandaled feet were sticking out from between the wind chests.

"Excuse me?" Tucker said.

A muffled voice came from beneath the organ. "Go away!"

"I'm looking for Father September," Tucker said.

More muttering. It sounded like Latin. A claw hammer and a wooden walking staff slid out from beneath the wind chests, followed by the rest of Father September, a robed, elderly man with long gray hair and a full white beard. Using his staff, he climbed painfully to his feet. His long mustard-colored robe was stained with dust and oil, his face crisscrossed with scars and spotted with age, his eyes set deeply in nests of wrinkles.

"Father September?" Tucker said.

Father September peered at Tucker, his brow furrowed. They stared at each other for several heartbeats, then the old man's eyes flared in sudden recognition.

"Curtis!"

The deep voice hit Tucker like a mallet striking a gong. He knew it well.

"Dad?" Tucker's voice cracked.

The old man's face went soft. "Tucker! I thought you were my brother come again."

Tucker stared. His father had become an old man.

"But it is truly you," said the Reverend Adrian Feye. He added, in a voice almost too soft for Tucker to hear, "As it is written." He sank to his knees and reached out with his arms.

Tucker took a step back.

The old man looked down at himself and spat out a bitter

laugh. "You are frightened. I cannot blame you." He used his staff to help himself stand. "Come." He gestured toward the sacristy. "There is much to discuss, and little time."

He used his staff to steady himself as he limped into the sacristy and lowered himself to the cot. He laid his staff on his lap. Tucker sat across from him on the wooden chair, a thousand questions fighting for his tongue.

The old man waited.

"I went to the house. I saw Mom," Tucker said.

The old man's eyes softened. "Did she know you?"

Tucker shook his head.

The old man sighed. "She does not remember me, either."

"What *happened* to her? How did she get so young? And you—how did you get so *old*?"

The old man smiled. Several of his teeth were missing. Tucker thought, *Can this really be my father?*

"When did you see me last?" his father asked.

"In the tomb. When you told me Mom was dead. When the soldiers came."

"The tomb. Yes. The soldiers . . ."

"I thought they were going to kill you!"

"As did I. They threw me into an oubliette—an underground cell so small that I could not spread my arms without touching the walls. I do not know how long I sat in the darkness with only vermin for company.

"I passed the time by addressing the vermin as I would my flock. I spoke the Gospels, the great stories of the New

Testament, first in Latin, then in Aramaic, and again in Greek. It seemed to calm the rats; they bit me less often. The fleas and lice were not so forbearing." He scratched a remembered itch. "I did not know at the time, but my words echoed through the shaft to where they could be heard by others. They gathered— the rats, the people—to hear my words. It was during those long, dark, endless days of hearing nothing but my own voice that I found God again."

"You believe in God now?"

"If not God, then who shepherded me through those dark times? The Medicants tore God from my heart, but I found Him again in the blackness, and yet again when the Romans dragged me out of the hole and nailed me to a cross."

"They crucified you?"

He displayed the knotted scars on his wrists. "Along with several others. I hung with thieves, runaway slaves, heretics, graverobbers. . . . It was a festive affair, much better attended than Josua's execution."

"Did you—? I mean, what happened?"

"Unlike Josua, the man you saw on the cross, I was saved. Josua never rose from the dead—he was too far gone for the Medicants' digital witchcraft." His voice took on a bitter edge. "Heartless drones, drowning themselves in digits and devices. The Medicants represent a dark path for mankind, Tuck, both as victims and carriers of the Plague."

"But how did you survive? You said you were crucified!"

"I was stolen from the cross by those who would become

my disciples. The Essenes. They had heard me preaching from the oubliette and recognized me as a vessel of the Lord even before I knew it myself.

"For weeks I lay in a morass of fever and pain, hidden deep within the house of a man called Yosef, willing my body to heal, speaking directly to God. They say that in my delirium, I spoke the Gospels — or rather, what would later become the Gospels. Yosef assigned a scribe to attend my every utterance. It came to pass that when I recovered, I understood that my purpose was to spread the Word.

"I traveled the Holy Land and spoke of things to come. Wherever I went, I was followed by a throng. It was not for many long years that I came to realize that those who followed me were far more righteous than I, for they had left their homes willingly, while I fed upon their adoration with all the narcissism of a false prophet. And so, as I felt myself entering my twilight years, I knew that I must become a seeker myself. I had my apostles raise me to the Gate on Golgotha. Standing upon their shoulders, I cast myself into the whorl. That was how I met the Master and how my eyes were truly opened."

"The Master?"

"Yes. He was waiting on the other side of the Gate. It was he who showed me the way. It was he who showed me that it is here in Hopewell that our great work must begin."

"Father September?" Brother Koan appeared in the doorway, hands clasped before his chest.

"Yes, Koan?"

"We should leave soon."

"A few moments, Koan."

Brother Koan nodded and withdrew. Father September's eyes lost focus; for a moment, he looked as if he was about to pass out.

"How come you call yourself Father September?" Tucker asked.

"Look at me." Father September spread his arms. "Who here would believe that I was once the Reverend Adrian Feye? Even if they did believe, it would only frighten them. I call myself September because September is when all things will change."

"You mean this September? Now?"

"Yes. You will see." The old man once again bestowed upon Tucker his frightful, gap-toothed smile.

"So who is this Master?"

"He who revealed to me that the roots of the Medicant curse lie here, in this time. I returned to a Hopewell filled with people walking the streets with wires coming out of their ears, communicating by pressing buttons with their thumbs, staring into tiny screens as if what they are seeing is real, turning their backs on what they once were, rushing headlong toward what they may become. We live in dreadful times."

"This is because you don't like computers and cell phones?"

"These digital devices . . . You have heard of the great plagues God visited upon Egypt? The greatest plague of all is upon us: the Digital Plague."

The Medicant woman, Tucker remembered, had said something about a plague. And so had Awn.

"The question is simply this," his father continued. "Is a future, once observed, still changeable? Or does the fact that we have observed it make it an immutable part of our personal past?" He pointed at Tucker's blue Medicant boots. "If we change our direction, will those boots suddenly disappear from your feet? I fear not, yet I know we must try. The seeds of Plague are planted deep. Your mother was one of its first victims. The Plague began—the Plague *begins*—here and now, in the Digital Age. Do you remember your mother working all those sudoku puzzles? It was sudoku that destroyed her.

"The Plague appears under many guises. Its victims are everywhere around us, but the disease goes unrecognized. They sometimes call it autism, sometimes Alzheimer's, sometimes depression. Sometimes they give it other names. The doctors and scientists are blinded by numbers; they do not see that it is the numbers themselves that are destroying us. We must return ourselves to a state of grace. No cell phones, no computers, no electronic devices feeding upon our senses, no falling upon the digital sword of technology. As it says in the Bible, *We dare not make ourselves of the number.*" He raised his staff and gazed out through the walls as if looking out over a great throng. His arm holding the staff began to shake. In a softer voice, he said, "I took your mother to the Medicants to be cured—to the very people who allowed the Plague to take root. I did not know any better. The Medicants could not help her. I thought her dead, but later I learned that they gave her to the Boggsians."

"Boggsians . . ." Tucker remembered Awn saying something about Boggsians being the builders of the diskos. She had called them Amish Jews.

"Yes, Boggsians. Unholy heretics. They command powerful digital technologies, and sell to any who can pay. They could not restore your mother, so they destroyed her."

"But . . . she's not dead."

"I fear she is, but she was reborn. I do not know what digital witchery the Boggsians employed, nor why, but the woman you met in our home was raised as a Pure Girl by the Lah Sept. She is Emily, but she is not our Emily — she is the Lamb Emma. I do not account for it, but I accept the blessing of her presence."

Tucker shook his head helplessly. The only part he understood was that his mother had forgotten him and that his father had become this strange old man.

"What about Lahlia?" he asked.

"The girl?" The old man frowned. "I know nothing of her."

Brother Koan appeared in the doorway again.

"Father?"

"Patience, Brother." Father September used his staff to help himself up. "Come, Tucker. We have our parts to play."

# 40    THE GREEN TENT

They rode to the county park in a black suv driven by Tamm, the man who had been in the house with his mother. Tamm seemed as surprised to see Tucker as Tucker was to see him, but he said nothing. Tucker and his father got in back, while Brother Koan took the passenger seat.

Tucker leaned close to his father and said in a low voice, "The guy driving? He was at our house with Mom."

"Tamm and Emma are married." He coughed out a bitter laugh. "He is, in a sense, your stepfather." He placed a hand on Tucker's wrist and squeezed. "You trust me, don't you?"

Tucker stared at his father. If he blurred his eyes, he could still see the Reverend Adrian Feye, who had once fished from their dock, carved wooden trolls, and built a church out of dreams and faith. But mostly he saw what his father had become.

A stranger.

*    *    *

Tucker hardly recognized Hopewell County Park. The entrance was now dominated by an enormous arch with the words *VERE RESURREXIT* carved across the top. The soccer field was trampled brown grass beneath an ocean of folding chairs. At the far end of the field stood a wooden platform about twenty feet high, with steps leading up to it on the front and sides, making it look like a stumpy five-sided pyramid. On top of the platform was a large dark-green tent, one curtained side facing the sea of chairs. Two men in yellow shirts were setting up more chairs at the far end of the field.

Brother Tamm drove across the field and around to the back, where an RV was parked. They climbed out of the SUV and were greeted by a man who looked like Brother Tamm's twin, with the same cap of curly black hair, the same dark eyes.

"Welcome, Father," he said, taking Father September's arm.

"Bless you, Brother Cort."

Tamm and Koan went out to the RV. Tucker followed his father and Brother Cort up the steps at the rear of the platform. The man pulled aside a flap in the rear of the tent. A familiar hum reached Tucker's ears.

"It is safe," said his father, beckoning Tucker forward. They entered the tent together.

Inside, the tent was dimly lit by the silvery glow of a disko. The disk was smaller than the others he had seen — only about three feet in diameter — and was framed by a pink fleshy-looking band. The smell of overheated plastic stung his nose.

"It is constrained," said his father. The pink band sur-rounding the disko was pierced by metal hooks at six equidis-tant points around its perimeter. The hooks were attached to taut wire cables, which were fastened to two heavy steel tent posts.

"This is where you get your miracles," said Tucker.

"It is an instrument, no more."

Tucker ducked under one of the cables to view the disko from the other side.

The back side of the disk was a pink fleshy lump with a deflated, wormlike tail hanging from its center.

His father joined him. "A tool of the Gnomon."

"Gnomon?"

"The Gnomon are a faction of the Klaatu. They seek to undo that which has been done. They built this thing."

Tucker's head was spinning. "I thought the Klaatu were like ghosts. How do they build stuff?"

"They employ Boggsians, who built this device at their behest. We have captured it, as you see."

The tent flap opened, briefly flooding the interior with sunlight. A sharp-featured, goateed man wearing a cream-colored three-piece suit entered the tent and said, "It is a *maggot.*"

The man in the suit walked around the disko and peered closely at Tucker. For a second, Tucker did not recognize him—and then he did. The last time he had looked into those coal-dark eyes, the man had had a scraggly beard and been wearing a long yellow robe.

"We meet again," said the priest. He reached out with his forefinger to touch the exact spot on Tucker's chest where a black stone blade had once torn open his heart.

## 41   MASTER GHEEN

Tucker tried to back away, but his father grasped his arm, saying, "It's all right, Tucker. This is Master Gheen."

"But he—"

"I know, I know," his father said. "That was an unfortunate misunderstanding."

"He tried to *kill* me!" Tucker said, yanking his arm free from his father's grasp. "Twice!"

Master Gheen's mouth drew back into a smile that was all teeth and no warmth. His voice matched his expression. "Forgive me, please. When you appeared upon the Cydonian Pyramid that night, we thought the both of you to be agents of the Gnomon. We would not knowingly harm the only son of our founder." He inclined his head toward Tucker's father.

Aghast, Tucker looked from Gheen to his father. "Founder?"

Father September nodded. "It is as I said. We all have our parts to play."

Tucker whirled on the man in the cream-colored suit. "And what's *his* part?" He moved toward Gheen, his hands clenched hard as rocks. "To *kill* people?"

Master Gheen held up his hands and backed away, still smiling.

"Tucker, *stop*!" his father said.

Tucker stopped.

Gheen spread his hands. "Whom have I killed?"

"You killed Awn!"

"The old woman? A Klaatu automaton."

"You tried to kill *me*!"

"And yet here you stand."

It was all Tucker could do to keep from punching him.

Tucker's father stepped between them. "Master, perhaps if I were to talk with my son alone?"

"As you wish," said Gheen, backing toward the exit.

After Gheen had left, Tucker's father let out a sigh. "He is not a bad man."

"He stabbed me with a knife."

"As Abraham attempted to slay Isaac."

"You're saying God told him to kill me?"

"As God allowed his own son to die upon the cross."

"I don't think God has anything to do with this. Why are you on this guy's side, anyway?"

"Master Gheen has shown me a dark future, son. When I left Golgotha, I arrived in the forest where the old woman lived—what they call the Terminus. Master Gheen was there, waiting. I traveled with him to the time of the Lah Sept in the city called Romelas. We arrived amid chaos. The city was burning. The temple was under attack by a mob of workers led by a one-eyed madwoman. We were able to fight through the mob and reach the temple, where the Master activated the temple defense mechanisms. Many died that day.

"It was in the temple that I found your mother reborn as the Lamb Emma. It was there, as we huddled, trapped amid the burning city, that Master Gheen taught me the true histories of the Lah Sept."

"Histories? Like more than one?"

"There are many paths. We choose our destiny."

"If it's our 'destiny,' we don't have much choice, do we?"

"The histories describe several futures. Our actions today will determine which of these futures comes to pass. Plague is with us now, but it need not consume us all. There is hope. We have many destinies; we choose among them."

Tucker remembered something Awn had said: *Choose well, and you may find yourself where you wish to be.*

"So what is this destiny?"

His father did not reply.

"It's not right," said Tucker. "None of this. Mom shouldn't be married to that guy, even if she can't remember us. Even if it's not really her."

"The Lamb Emma is young. I am old. She has a new life. As for whether she is truly Emily, I believe her soul remains a constant. It is for her sake, and others like her, that I am here."

From outside, they could hear faint voices and the clatter of folding chairs being shifted. The tent flap opened. Master Gheen entered again, followed by Brother Koan and Brother Tamm. All three of them were wearing yellow robes.

Tucker's insides turned to jelly. He felt as if he was back on the pyramid about to get his chest ripped open.

A rumbling sound, like distant thunder, came from outside the tent.

"Why don't you just go back to your stupid pyramid." Tucker hoped his fear wasn't showing in his voice.

"So we shall." Master Gheen pressed his palms together and performed a shallow, mocking bow. "But first you must perform a small task for us."

"I'm not doing anything for you," Tucker said.

The distant thunder became the rumble of an engine. Tamm and Koan moved closer to Tucker, hemming him in. The rumbling suddenly stopped. They could hear angry voices, then a thud followed by a shout of pain. Master Gheen frowned and motioned with his hand. Tamm stepped over to the tent flap and peeked outside.

"Master, there is —" Someone grabbed the front of Tamm's robe and yanked him out of the tent. This was followed by a series of thumps — Tucker pictured him tumbling down the steps.

A girl with yellow hair and a shiny black vest stepped into the tent. Her dark eyes flicked efficiently from Gheen to the yellow-robed acolytes to Tucker's father to the maggot and finally to Tucker.

"Tucker Feye. You live," Lahlia said with a small, tight smile.

## 42 THE MAGGOT

LAHLIA LOOKED OLDER THAN HE REMEMBERED — SHE had matured as much as he had, maybe even more. She was taller and more solid-looking, her features had hardened slightly, and she had a thin white scar running down her left cheek. Even more striking, she radiated competence, as if she knew exactly what she wanted and what she had to do to get it.

Koan moved toward Lahlia and tried to grab her. She ducked under his arm and delivered a vicious kick to the side of his knee with her thick-soled black boot. Tucker heard something snap; Koan fell with a gasp.

"Master *Gheen*," Lahlia said, making his name sound like something unclean.

Gheen took a step back. "Do I know you?"

Lahlia gave the priest a withering look. She touched a forefinger to the corner of her left eye, then slowly traced the thin scar down her cheek to where it ended at her jaw.

"Did you think you were rid of me, *priest*?" The contempt in her voice was unmistakable.

Master Gheen's eyes widened, and his mouth fell open.

Lahlia shifted her eyes to Tucker's father. "Reverend Feye, you have aged."

Tucker's father simply stared at her, too startled or confused to reply.

Tucker said, "How did you get here? How did—?"

Lahlia cut him off. "We must go. If you wish to live."

"He *lives* to fulfill his destiny," said Gheen. "As it is written."

"In your precious *Book of September*?" Lahlia said with a curl of her lip. "You *priests* care only to perpetuate your own twisted history."

"And what do you know? You are a *Yar*."

"And you are a *priest,* priest." She turned to Tucker. "In *his* history, you die. You are murdered by your own father and fed to the Timesweep." She pointed at the maggot.

"Do not listen to this lying *Yar*," said Gheen.

Tucker looked from Gheen to his father, aghast. "You were going to kill me?"

"As it is written," his father echoed Master Gheen's words, refusing to meet Tucker's eyes.

"To be *resurrected*," said Gheen. "To become a prophet. To bring peace and—"

A rapid series of thuds and gasps came from just outside the tent. The flap jerked aside, and Kosh entered. "Those guys just don't know how to stay down when they been punched," he said, quickly scanning the tent and doing a double take when his eyes landed on Tucker.

"Kid!" he said, his eyes softening. He stepped toward Tucker as if to give him a hug. Koan moaned piteously from the floor, staring with dismay at his knee, which was bending in the wrong direction. Kosh and Tucker both looked at him. Gheen, seeing his chance, reached for something within his robes.

Tucker had seen that move before, in the meadow outside Awn's cabin. He was in motion even before the silver cylinder cleared the priest's robe. The weapon snapped out to its full length, pointing directly at Kosh. Tucker knocked the priest's arm up. A jet of energy spouted from the weapon, blasting a ragged slash in the roof of the tent. Gheen cried out in rage, swinging the extended cylinder like a club. Tucker ducked under it, grabbed the weapon on the backswing, and yanked it from Gheen's grasp. He backed away, trying to figure out how to activate it.

Gheen, his face contorted with fury, threw himself at Tucker. Kosh stepped in and hammered his fist into the side of Gheen's neck. The priest clutched his throat and dropped to his knees, gasping.

Kosh looked at Tucker and grinned. "Should've known I wasn't rid of you, kid."

Lahlia, looking up at the smoking hole in the canvas, said, "The others will have noticed that. Time to go."

Tucker's father was standing beside the maggot, looking ancient and powerless. Gheen groaned and started to get up, saw the weapon in Tucker's hands, and froze. Tucker located a small stud near the base of the cylinder. He rested his thumb on it.

Lahlia said, "That is a Lah Sept *arma*. Be careful where you point it."

"How about if I keep it pointed at him?" Tucker said, aiming the weapon at Gheen.

"That would be good," said Lahlia.

"Please," Gheen said in a hoarse voice, displaying empty hands as he slowly stood up. "I mean you no harm."

"Shoot him if he moves," Lahlia said in a flat voice. She stepped over to the tent flap and looked outside.

Kosh said, "Maybe we should just shoot him anyway."

"Curtis, you have no idea what you are dealing with," said Tucker's father.

"Do I know you, old man?"

"You don't recognize your own brother?"

Kosh's jaw fell slowly open. "Adrian?"

Father September nodded. "There are forces at work that you cannot understand, my brother."

"I'll say. Look at you. How'd you get all . . . *ancient*?"

"Curtis, I—"

Lahlia interrupted him. "More men are coming this way. We must leave *now*."

Tucker hesitated, looking at Master Gheen and his father, questions swirling through his head. What had happened to his father, that he would consider killing his only son? Gheen claimed Tucker would be resurrected as a prophet. What did that mean? And how—?

"If you stay, you'll be killed," Lahlia said.

And how had Lahlia gotten older and so . . . so *bossy*?

"We wish only what is best for all," Gheen said to Tucker. "Ask your father." He took a step toward Tucker.

Tucker pressed the stud and blasted a hole in the wooden platform in front of Gheen's feet. The priest stopped. An instant later, the flap was yanked aside and Ronnie Becker, wearing a yellow T-shirt, strode into the tent.

"Ronnie. Thank God it's you," Kosh said.

Ronnie smiled and raised his hand. Tucker saw the baton too late to warn Kosh. The baton crackled, and Kosh collapsed.

Tucker swung the *arma* toward Ronnie, but Gheen grabbed his arm, wrestling for the weapon. Tucker tore the *arma* free and clubbed Gheen on the side of the head. The priest staggered back. Lahlia was grappling with Ronnie, trying to wrest the baton from his grip. Tucker pointed the *arma* at them. Lahlia saw him and jumped back.

"Stop!" Tucker shouted.

Ronnie ignored him and thrust the baton at Lahlia. Tucker pressed the stud on the *arma*. Ronnie's knee exploded—he dropped the baton and toppled with a ghastly shriek. The bottom half of his left leg remained standing upright.

Tucker, horrified, stared at the leg as it wavered, then tipped onto its side. The charred-hot-dog smell of incinerated flesh filled the tent. Tucker's stomach clenched.

"No more, Tucker!" His father's voice echoed in the tent. Tucker felt as if he was about to vomit. His grip on the *arma* loosened.

"Tucker!" Lahlia shouted.

Before Tucker could react, the *arma* was ripped from his hands.

"Do not move." Gheen backed off a few steps, keeping the *arma* pointed in Lahlia and Tucker's direction. Ronnie Becker moaned and fell silent.

"Send Brother Ron through the Gate," Gheen said to Tucker's father.

Father September dragged the unconscious Ronnie over to the pulsing maggot. The stump of Ronnie's leg left a thick trail of blood. Half lifting him, he tipped Ronnie into the maggot's disko.

"Let's not forget the leg," said Gheen. He picked up the severed leg by the ankle and tossed it into the maggot. The leg disappeared in an orange flash.

"The Yar, too," said Gheen, looking at Lahlia.

"No!" Tucker said.

Gheen pointed the *arma* at Kosh, who was lying senseless on the floor. "It is not necessary that he live."

Tucker met Lahlia's eyes. She nodded. Her eyes shifted quickly to Kosh, then to Gheen.

"I will do as you say," she said. Tucker glanced at Kosh and noticed that his eyes were open and alert. Lahlia made a slight motion with one hand, telling Tucker to wait. Gheen still had the *arma* trained on Kosh, but his eyes were locked on Lahlia. Kosh winked at Tucker as Lahlia moved slowly toward the maggot.

"Quickly," said Gheen.

"It was good to see you, Tucker Feye," Lahlia said, looking Tucker right in the eye. "Do not hesitate."

"Go *now,*" said Gheen.

"I will see you later as well, *priest,*" Lahlia said. "As it is *written.*" She smiled humorlessly. "In *my* history, *priest,* I send you to hell."

Gheen snarled and swung the *arma* toward Lahlia as she dove into the disko. The instant the priest moved the weapon away from Kosh, Tucker was in motion, driving his shoulder into Gheen's side. A jet of flame seared the floor and ripped open the side of the tent. The weapon flew from Gheen's hands. Kosh leaped to his feet and snatched the *arma* from midair as Tucker slammed the priest into one of the steel tent posts anchoring the maggot.

Kosh triggered the *arma,* aiming high to avoid hitting Tucker. The tent post just above their heads turned cherry red and exploded in a mist of molten metal. Gheen screamed as the superheated droplets rained down on them. They jumped back from the post, their garments sending up tendrils of smoke. The canvas sagged. The maggot, with one side of its bindings gone slack, began to pulse and twitch.

Gheen made a dash for the doorway, frantically brushing hot metal fragments from his robe. Tucker launched himself and tackled him from behind. The priest fell headlong and hit the floor with his face. Kosh grabbed the baton Ronnie had dropped, jabbed it against Gheen's neck. The priest convulsed, then lay still.

Kosh looked at Tucker. "You okay?"

Tucker nodded and climbed to his feet. His coveralls were spotted with burn marks from the hot metal. "You sure recovered quick," he said, gesturing at the baton in Kosh's hand.

Kosh touched the handle end of the baton to his heavy leather jacket. "My leathers must've blocked most of its juice."

Tucker's father, still standing beside the damaged maggot, said, "Curtis . . . what have you done?"

The maggot hissed and sputtered.

"What have *I* done?" Kosh looked from his brother to Gheen, then at Tucker. "Adrian, what happened to you?"

"I have seen the future."

"Yeah? Then how come you didn't know this was going to happen?" Kosh shook his head in disgust. He strode to the front of the tent to look outside. "We better get going," he said to Tucker.

"No. We have to wait for Lahlia."

"We don't know she's coming back, kid. She could be anywhere from Abilene to Timbuktu." He was still looking out the tent flap. "There's another SUV coming, and those two guys I put down are waking up again. We got to go."

"I can't," Tucker said.

"Why not?"

Tucker was staring at the maggot. "Lahlia. She came here for me. And I want to meet these Gnomon, or Boggsians, or whatever. Maybe there's something they can do. Or undo."

"You got no idea what happens, you jump into that thing. Look at it."

The maggot's disko was slightly out of round, and the pink flesh surrounding it was pulsing.

"I can't *not* go after her," Tucker said.

Kosh shook his head slowly. "You got heart, kid."

"My name is Tucker."

"Tucker. You *still* got heart."

For a moment, Tucker thought his uncle might try to stop him, but instead Kosh said, "I'm going with you."

"No," Tucker said. "You have to stay. My mom is here."

"Emily? Here? Where?"

"She was at the house. She's married to one of *them.* I think they got her brainwashed or something. You have to make her remember."

"Remember what?" Kosh said.

"Us," Tucker said.

Kosh nodded slowly. "I can do that." With the *arma* in one hand and the baton in the other, he looked ready to take on an army.

"Son"—Father September, his voice pleading and desperate, held out his hands—"do not turn your back on your destiny!"

*"Destiny?"* Tucker looked at the strange old man standing

before him. A man who had once been his father. A man who wanted to kill him. A distressing stew of emotions rose up within him—disgust, pity, anger, and above all, sorrow for all he had lost—but beneath it all was a sense of what he had to do. "My *destiny* is what *I* make of it."

Tucker turned his back to his father and leaped into the maggot's maw.

**43 THE CHOSEN**

MASTER GHEEN AWAKENED TO THE SPUTTER AND BUZZ of the maggot-borne Gate. His head was pounding. His teeth hurt. A wave of nausea rolled up his abdomen. Gheen turned his head to the side and vomited. He wiped his mouth with his sleeve and looked up. Father September was standing over him.

"What happened?" he croaked.

"They are gone, Master."

"The boy?"

Father September gestured toward the maggot. Brother Tamm was repairing the armature that confined it, reattaching the slackened cables.

"He followed the Yar into the Gate. He has not returned."

"Then it is as we feared. He is truly a danger to us all." Gheen closed his eyes, took a fortifying breath, and attempted to stand. Tamm moved to help him, but Gheen waved him back.

It was important to appear strong, even in circumstances such as these. Slowly, he got to his feet on his own.

"What of your brother?" he asked.

"He goes to seek out the Lamb Emma," Father September said.

Tamm's face darkened. He ran out of the tent.

"Do not spare him," Gheen called after him. "He is nothing."

Gheen moved to the front of the tent and looked out past the curtain. The numberless multitude was waiting, seated on the sea of folding chairs, staring expectantly up at the platform. He fought off another wave of nausea, wondering how long he had been unconscious.

"The Lambs grow restless," he said. "History must be made real."

"How?" said Father September. "My son is gone."

"We must choose another." From within his robes, he produced a folded cloth. He opened it to reveal a black, wedge-shaped stone dagger.

Father September took the knife in his hand and tested the edge with his thumb. The blade, sharper than any razor, sliced easily through his skin. A glistening bead of blood welled from his thumb, broke, and trickled down his wrist. "An obsidian blade," he said. "A dark stone for a dark deed."

"One must pass through night to reach the dawn. Are you able?"

Father September nodded. "As it is written."

Tom Krause was sitting with several other Pure Boys near the steps leading up to the stage. The crowd was restless — they had been gathered for nearly an hour, but nothing was happening. He leaned over the back of his chair and looked at the row of Pure Girls sitting behind them.

"What do you think is going on?" he asked Kathy Aamodt.

Kathy shook her head. She looked as impatient as Tom felt, but even with that tight frown, she was the most beautiful girl Tom had ever seen. In fact, she was the whole reason he had joined up with the Lambs.

He said, "You want a soda or something? I'm thirsty." A concession trailer had been set up near the entrance to the park. He figured he could get there and back in a few minutes, and who knew how long it would be before the show — or whatever — started.

"We're not supposed to talk," Kathy said.

The problem with Kathy was that she was too devout. She actually believed in all the miracles. Not that the miracles weren't impressive, but Tom secretly agreed with his father — anybody could make predictions and get lucky once in a while. He wondered what sort of tricks they would be witnessing today. Several people in wheelchairs were lining up in front of the platform. Maybe Father September would coax a few of them to walk again.

"You want to maybe go out to Hardy Lake after? We got a great rope swing."

She shushed him. Frustrated, Tom turned and found himself facing an acolyte wearing a yellow robe. The man pointed his forefinger at Tom.

"Me?" said Tom, trying to look innocent.

"Come," said the man, crooking his finger. "You are chosen."

# ACKNOWLEDGMENTS

*I received a lot of help with this book from some very generous readers, including, in approximate order of geotemporal proximity, Mary Logue, Tobias Ball, Joe Hautman, Tucker Foley, Kathy Erickson, Ellen Hart, Deborah Woodworth, Bill Smith, Karin Gilbertson, Jennifer Flannery, Jen Yoon, and Jonathan Coran (whose surname I fear I have misspelled). Thank you all.*

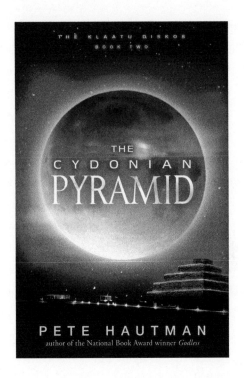

HALF A MILLENNIUM IN THE FUTURE, Lah Lia is a
protected and pampered Pure Girl raised in the shadow
of the Cydonian Pyramid. In return for a life of luxury,
Lah Lia must one day ascend the pyramid to be sacrificed
by the priests of Romelas and hurled bleeding into one of
the mysterious Gates — diskos — that hover around the
pyramid's top.

Lia believes she is prepared.

*Continue reading for a peak into* The Cydonian Pyramid,
*book two of the Klaatu Diskos* . . .

THE IRON STEPS WENT UP FOREVER, following the close walls of a cylindrical shaft, as the drugged tea in Lia's belly spread through her body. Her hair was crawling; her limbs belonged to someone else. She followed Master Gheen up the winding staircase, the other priests following close behind. Feet struck iron with the regularity of a funeral dirge. Time stretched and flexed.

They reached the top of the staircase. Master Gheen worked a lever on the wall of the shaft. Above them, the ceiling slid aside with a labored, grating rumble. They lifted her up the last few steps and emerged onto the frustum. A yellow moon hung high in the sky, the shadow of the earth nibbling at its margin. The crowded zocalo spread out on every side. A sea of upturned faces pitched and wavered; torches flickered; the opening to the stairway juddered shut.

Above each facet of the pyramid there hovered a swirling disk of gray. Lia tried to figure out which Gate was which, but her drug-addled mind failed her. Not that it mattered — the priests would choose for her.

With a priest on each arm, Lah Lia was paraded around the perimeter of the frustum. Showing her to the crowd. *You must remain aware.* Aware? Her limbs were numb, her thoughts muddled. She felt herself being lifted and placed upon the altar, an impossibly large block of pure black obsidian. She tried to remember what Yar Song had told her to do. Twist to the side? She tried to sit up, but one of the priests pushed her back down with the butt end of his stun baton. She stared up at the moon, at the shadow biting into it. As the priests babbled their ritual

*An excerpt from* The Cydonian Pyramid

phrases, the pale yellow of the moon deepened, then turned slowly to rust, as the shadow of the earth advanced across its surface. The blood moon.

A bright green flash erupted from one of the Gates, producing a startled shout from the nearest priest. Lah Lia looked in time to see a man fly out of the Gate and land face-first on the frustum. The man was oddly dressed in garments of faded indigo. He pushed himself up onto his knees and looked straight at her with eyes of blue. Lia had never seen a grown man with blue eyes. Male throwbacks were culled or given to the Boggsians as infants, never to be seen again.

"Who are you, and why have you blasphemed this holy place?" Master Gheen demanded of him.

The man, clearly confused and frightened, responded in some strange dialect and rose to his feet. Master Gheen looked past him to one of the other priests, who attempted to grab the man. The stranger dodged him and backed away around the edge of the frustum. The other priest came around from the opposite side and jammed his baton into the man's back. The man's arms flew out to the sides, and he fell, quivering, to the frustum. The priest applied the baton again, and again, until the man lay as if dead.

While the priests' attention was on the intruder, Lia had climbed to her feet. The drugged tea slowed her, but her muscles did as she asked. Not that there was much she could do with them. There was no way off the pyramid other than to climb down the sides into the crowd, and this crowd had come

*An excerpt from* The Cydonian Pyramid

to see her sacrificed. The priests were grouped around the fallen man. Lia looked at each of the shimmering Gates, trying to figure out which was which.

She was staring at the Gate the man had come through when it flashed green and expelled a small gray furry creature. It landed on its feet. A kitten! The tiny cat crouched and hissed.

The Gate flashed again. A boy tumbled out and landed on his hands and knees, facing away from her. He sat back, looking out over the zocalo, then stood up and turned around. He had blue eyes, like the man. Another throwback!

The kitten jumped from the frustum to the altar, then from the altar into Lia's arms. Reflexively, she caught the small cat and hugged it to her chest.

*"Mrrp?"* the kitten said.

The boy's attention turned to the priests and to the blue-clad man. He ran toward them, shouting something. Master Gheen pulled a baton from within his robes. Lia knew she would never have another chance. The boy dodged Master Gheen's baton thrust, grabbed one of the torchères, and pulled it from its base. The priests were coming at him from every side; the boy swung the torchère, hitting one of the priests and knocking him over the edge. The priest tumbled, screaming, down the side of the pyramid. Master Gheen struck the torch pole with his baton, snapping it in half.

Yar Song's words came to Lia once again: *If you wish to live, you must take every opportunity, no matter how slim, to alter your fate.*

*An excerpt from* The Cydonian Pyramid